THE GROOMING OF
Alice

Books by Phyllis Reynolds Naylor

THE GROOMING OF
Alice

Phyllis

Reynolds

Naylor

A Jean Karl Book

Atheneum Books for Young Readers
NEW YORK · LONDON · TORONTO · SYDNEY · SINGAPORE

○─○─○─○

Atheneum Books for Young Readers
An imprint of Simon & Schuster Children's Publishing Division
1230 Avenue of the Americas
New York, New York 10020

Book design by Nina Barnett
The text of this book is set in Berkeley Oldstyle.
Printed in the United States of America
4 6 8 10 9 7 5 3

Library of Congress Cataloging-in-Publication Data
Naylor, Phyllis Reynolds.
The grooming of alice / Phyllis Reynolds Naylor.—1st ed.   p.   cm.
"A Jean Karl book."
Summary: During the summer between eighth and ninth grades, Alice and her
friends Pamela and Elizabeth decide to improve themselves through exercise.
ISBN 0-689-82633-8
[1. Friendship Fiction. 2. Body image Fiction. 3. Self-perception
Fiction. 4. Summer Fiction.] I. Title.
PZ7.N24Gt 2000   [Fic]-dc21   99-32184

To Lindsey Hundt
and her daughter, Julia Horwitz,
with thanks for all their help

CONTENTS

The Program

"It's going to be one of the most exciting summers of our lives," Pamela used to tell Elizabeth and me whenever we thought about the summer between eighth and ninth grades. "All the stupid things we've ever done will be behind us, and all the *wonderful* stuff will be waiting to happen."

But now, on the first day of vacation, as the three of us stood in our bathing suits in front of the full-length mirror in Elizabeth's bedroom, we realized that the same bodies were going into high school along with us, the same faults, the same personalities, some of the same problems we'd had before.

Elizabeth, with her long dark hair and lashes, her gorgeous skin, broke the silence first. "I'm *fat!*" she said in dismay. "*Look* at me!"

We looked. She was the same beautiful Elizabeth she'd always been, except that her face and arms were slightly rounder, but she was pointing to her thighs, which puffed out just a little below her suit.

"Saddlebags! I have saddlebag thighs!" she cried. "My legs look like jodhpurs!"

They didn't, of course, but before I could say a word, I heard murmurs on the other side of me coming from Pamela. Pamela is pretty, too, though not as drop-dead beautiful as Elizabeth. She's naturally blond, and wears her hair in a short feather-cut, like Peter Pan. It always seemed to me as though Pamela Jones had the perfect figure, but it didn't seem that way to Pamela.

"I have absolutely no definition," she observed.

"Huh?" I said. Were these girls nuts?

"My arms and legs are like pudding! One part looks the same as the rest."

"Pamela, *anyone* can tell your arm from your leg," I told her.

"But you can't tell what's fat and what's muscle!"

I couldn't believe what I was hearing. "People just want to look at you, Pamela. They don't want to *dissect* you!"

Pamela, however, meant business. "Well, I certainly need to do some toning," she said.

"And *I* want to lose this fat," said Elizabeth. "What do *you* want to change, Alice?"

Friends, I thought. But I just took a good, long look at myself in the mirror and thought about it.

I've got the same color hair as my mom had, they tell me—strawberry blond. Mom died when I was small, and I don't remember much about her, but they say she was tall and liked to sing. I'm more on the short side, and can't even carry a tune. I'm not fat, but I'm not thin. I'm more plain than I am pretty, but I'm not ugly. Miss Average, that's me.

"I don't know," I said finally. "What do you guys think I should change?"

You should never ask anyone that. You're just begging for worries you never had before.

"Well, if you want an honest opinion, your waist is a little thick, Alice," said Elizabeth. One thing about Elizabeth, she's loyal to a fault. You ask her to tell you something, she tells.

"And your legs are too straight," said Pamela. "I mean, you don't have to be ashamed of them or anything, but your calves hardly have any curve."

"Your breasts could be a little fuller," said Elizabeth. "Of course, they're bigger than mine . . . ."

"And your arms have no definition at all," Pamela finished.

It's really weird, you know? Five minutes before, I had put on my bathing suit, ready to go over to Mark Stedmeister's pool with the gang, feeling really good about myself and my friends, and suddenly I was disintegrating before my very eyes! I had this new royal blue bathing suit that looked great with my hair, and now nothing looked right.

"There's only one solution," said Pamela. "We've got to start an exercise program. We've got exactly two and a half months to get ourselves in shape before school begins. Because how ever you look when you start ninth grade, that's how people will think of you for the next four years."

Now *that* was a sobering thought. I don't know where Pamela comes up with stuff like this, but she's got a cousin in New Jersey who knows all about what they think in New York, so we learn a lot from her. What we don't get from Pamela's cousin, I get from my cousin Carol in Chicago, who's two years older than Lester, my brother, and used to be married to a sailor.

I'd never seen Pamela quite so gung ho as she was now.

"If we get up at seven each morning for the next ten weeks . . . ," she began.

"Seven!" I wailed.

"Well, eight, maybe. And we jog for three miles . . ."

"In public?" Elizabeth gasped.

We stared. One reason we like Elizabeth is that her whole world sort of spins on a different axis.

"I suppose we *could* jog nine hundred times around your room, if you'd prefer," Pamela said dryly. "But if we spend the next ten weeks jogging every morning with ankle weights, and do push-ups, we might look reasonably good by the time we start high school. And no ice cream. No chips. No Oreos or anything like that."

I looked first at Pamela and then at Elizabeth. No ice cream, no chips, and jogging three miles with ankle weights? This was a *summer*?

Elizabeth shook her head. "I don't want anyone to see me sweat," she declared.

"If you jog, you're going to sweat, Elizabeth!" Pamela told her. "You have to sweat! You're *supposed* to sweat! If you don't sweat, the fat will stay right there, and you'll keep those saddlebag thighs forever."

I looked at Elizabeth's face and wished Pamela hadn't said that. It's one thing to talk about saddlebags yourself, but something else to hear your friends say it.

"Oh, come on!" I said, grabbing Elizabeth's beach towel and tying it around her waist. "Let's go on over to Mark's. Everybody's waiting."

Everybody was. We've been hanging out at Mark Stedmeister's pool for the last few summers, and even after Pamela and Mark broke up for the second time, we still go over there. Pamela went with Brian for a while after that, and then she wouldn't go out with either one of them, and now the guys have sort of lost interest. We're still all good friends, though.

Patrick Long, my boyfriend, was there, and Justin Collier, who likes Elizabeth. Except for Patrick and me, though, we don't couple-off the way we used to. Right after sixth grade, "couples" were "in." Most of us had never had boy or girl friends before, so everyone wanted one and found someone to hold hands with, whether they liked each other or not. Now we mostly do things as a group, and only Patrick and I are still "going together."

"Heeey! The babes!" Brian yelled when he saw us, and we smiled. A year ago, there would have been sheer terror beneath my smile, because I'd been deathly afraid of deep water, only nobody knew it, not even Dad. It wasn't until I'd confided in my twenty-one-year-old brother that I learned to swim the deep end, when Les took me to a pool and helped me swim across one corner of it.

Elizabeth and Pamela and I dropped our towels on a deck chair and dived in. Elizabeth went first because she wanted to hide her thighs, I went next because I didn't really care, and Pamela was the last one in because she wanted to show off her bright red bikini with the halter top. Patrick dived in the other end and came up the same time I did. We swam over to the other side of the pool together, and he kissed me on the eyelids before he was off again to play water basketball with Mark. That's what's nice about having a boyfriend. He's sort of always there, someone to count on. Not that I didn't look at other guys too, of course.

We horsed around in the water for a while, and when we came out and were all sitting around drinking Sprite, the talk was about summer jobs and what we had lined up. Now that some of us were fourteen, we could get work permits if we wanted.

Patrick was going to work for a landscaper loading trucks, pulling weeds and stuff. Brian had a job in a doughnut shop, Mark was shelving books at the library, and Justin Collier got a part-time job in a pizza place.

Of the girls, two of us were volunteering. Karen was helping out her aunt in a home for senior citizens, and I was going to be a candy striper at one of the hospitals, besides working in my dad's music store on Saturday mornings. Jill was going to summer school, and Elizabeth's mom was going to pay her to watch her baby brother four hours a day.

"What about you, Pamela?" someone asked.

She just shrugged. "I'll think of something," she said. Pamela was the only one who didn't have a clue. Her life was all torn up because her mom had run off with a boyfriend. It was as though the only thing Pamela could control anymore was her body, which was why she was devoting the next ten weeks to it, I think.

"Remember when all we had to do each summer was lie around the pool and play badminton?" Mark said, reaching for the chips. Elizabeth and Pamela and I wouldn't even look at the bowl. We tried to tune out all that crunching and munching.

"You make us sound like old people," said Patrick. *"Remember back in the olden days . . . ?"* Patrick's a redhead, and when he's out in the sun, the fine hair on his legs and arms looks orange, too.

Brian put his arms beneath his head and stared up at the clouds. "Yeah, back in the good old days the only thing we had to do was listen for the Good Humor Man. That was the high point of our day."

"Good old summertime!" said Justin, rolling over on Elizabeth's towel and tickling the bottoms of her feet. She kept giggling and drawing her feet up, and then he began playfully poking at her—her legs, her back, her stomach—and she kept trying to grab his hand.

"Hey, getting a little chubby, are we?" he asked jokingly as he poked at the space between her bathing suit top and bottom.

Elizabeth stopped laughing and sat up. "What do you mean?" she asked.

"Nothing," said Justin, grinning at her lazily. "You're just a little softer in all the right places."

But Elizabeth's face was pink. Mark, of course, who's about as subtle as a neon sign, had to say, "It's all those Good Humor bars, the kind with the chocolate bar in the center."

"It is *not!*" Elizabeth declared.

"I like the toasted almond bars," said Brian. "I could eat those all day." And the guys immediately started talking about their favorite ice cream, oblivious of what was happening with Elizabeth.

She sat stiffly on her towel, arms circling her thighs and calves, as though trying to shield her body from view. She wouldn't even touch the rest of her Sprite, and finally went in the house to change. I followed.

"Elizabeth, don't take what Justin said so seriously. You know you get a little puffy right before your period," I told her.

"I'm *fat!*" Elizabeth insisted.

"You're only round, not angular. Girls are *supposed* to be round."

"Fat!" said Elizabeth. "I'm F-A-T, as in whale blubber, walrus blubber, globules of lard all coagulating inside my body. F-A-T, as in pork roast, lamb chops, sausage, and leg of mutton."

"We don't want to *eat* you! We like you just the way you are," I told her.

But she marched into the Stedmeisters' bathroom and closed the door.

I put my face against the door frame. "Any weight you gained over the winter, you'll lose this summer by swimming and stuff," I called.

But when she came out, she was staring straight ahead. "I'm fat," she said again. "I will never eat another bite until I've lost fifteen pounds." And with a quick good-bye to the group, she left.

Pamela called the next morning to be sure I was ready to go running. She said that Elizabeth had been up since seven, and we were going to do three miles around the neighborhood. She'd already mapped it out.

I put on my sweatpants and a wrinkled T-shirt, Pamela arrived in short shorts and a top, and we crossed the street to pick up Elizabeth.

We hardly recognized her. She came out on the porch in sweatpants and a sweat jacket with sleeves that hung down below her hands. The hood of the jacket completely covered her hair and was tied under the chin. She was also wearing a huge pair of sunglasses. It was impossible to tell whether the creature beneath all that paraphernalia was male or female.

"Good grief, Elizabeth!" I said. "It's about seventy degrees outside. It's going up to eighty-three. We're not going sledding, you know."

"I don't want anyone to recognize me," Elizabeth said.

"Sure. They'll see Pamela and me and say, 'Hmmm. I wonder who that third person could be?' We've only been hanging around together since sixth grade," I told her.

There was simply no reasoning with her, so we started off, trying to find a pace that was right for the three of us.

"How many calories do you figure we burn in a half hour?" Elizabeth panted.

"It depends how fast we run. Enough to burn off a scoop of Häagan-Dazs, maybe," Pamela said. "Of course, if you add fudge sauce to that, and whipped cream . . ."

Elizabeth ran all the faster, but Pamela was in better shape than any of us, probably because her mom's boyfriend is a NordicTrack instructor and her mom's been getting herself in shape. In shape to move away with him, I guess, because they went to Colorado and were talking about opening a ski shop. Pamela's staying here with her dad, though. It's hard to get her to talk about it anymore. I think one of the reasons she runs is to work off all that anger.

We'd just turned the corner and were starting up the next block when Elizabeth suddenly covered her face. "Oh, my gosh, it's Justin's dad!" she cried. "Alice, get in front of me quick!"

I stared. "Elizabeth, it's just a *car!* His dad isn't even looking this way, and if he was, he wouldn't recognize you! *No*body would recognize you, not even your mother!"

The car turned at the next corner, and Elizabeth gave a sigh of relief. I thought maybe the silliness was over for a while, and we ran another block, but then suddenly Elizabeth disappeared. Just vanished, as though she'd fallen down a manhole.

"*Now* what?" said Pamela.

We stopped and looked around. Elizabeth was gone. And then we saw her foot sticking out from beneath a hedge. We knelt down and poked at her.

"Go *away!*" she shrieked. "Didn't you see? Brian's coming!"

I looked up the street. Brian was coming down the hill on his bike, heading for his job at the doughnut shop, I supposed.

"So?" I said. "He's going to work."

"He'll tell Justin how awful I look! How awful I *smell!* Just *go!* I *mean* it!" Elizabeth screeched.

Brian, of course, stopped to see what Pamela and I were looking at, and saw Elizabeth lying under the hedge.

"What happened? She get run over?" he asked, quickly wheeling his bike across the sidewalk.

"Not exactly," Pamela told him.

Brian came closer and squatted down beside Elizabeth. "Maybe you should call 911," he said anxiously. He reached out to take her pulse, and suddenly Elizabeth scrambled to her feet and started to run, Brian staring after her.

We followed, but could hardly keep up. She didn't stop till she'd reached my front porch, and the three of us collapsed in a heap on the steps.

"Well, that . . . should have been good . . . for at least two hundred calories," Pamela huffed. "Why don't you just wear a rubber raincoat, Elizabeth, so your sweat can't evaporate? Then *no* one will recognize you, and the fat will absolutely pour off."

Lester came out on the porch with a cup of coffee. "I *thought* I heard voices out here," he said. "Since when did *you* start getting up so early in the morning, Al?"

My full name is Alice Kathleen McKinley, but Dad and Lester call me Al. He looked at me, then Pamela, and then his eye fell on Elizabeth. She still wouldn't take off the hood of her jacket, and her dark glasses were all steamed up.

"Who is *that?*" he asked. "*What* is that?"

"Elizabeth," I told him. "She doesn't want anyone to see her sweat."

"She doesn't want anything to jiggle," Pamela said.

"She doesn't want anyone to hear her pant," I added.

Lester studied Elizabeth some more. "Hey, kiddo, if it doesn't sweat, jiggle, or pant, it's not alive," he said, "and I'm outta here." And he went back inside.

2

The Long Good-bye

When Dad came home from work the next day, he went straight upstairs and took a shower. I was hoping he'd grill shrimp or something for dinner, but when he came back down, he was wearing a shirt that Sylvia Summers had given him for Christmas, and the kind of aftershave that makes you want to follow the scent. I knew he must have a date with my former English teacher.

"Doing something special with Miss Summers?" I asked, noticing how well he had trimmed his nails and mustache.

"I guess you could call it that," Dad said. "I'm driving her to the airport. She leaves for England tonight."

I pressed the mute button on the remote and stared at him. I didn't know if I had actually been so wrapped up in myself that I'd forgotten about Dad and Miss Summers or whether it was something I just didn't want to think about. About how much he loved her, and how—I think—she loves him, too. Except that there's somebody else involved—Jim Sorringer, our vice principal from junior high school—whom she'd thought she was going to marry until she met Dad. So now she's going to England as an exchange teacher for a year to help her decide which one she likes best. I used to feel I couldn't stand it if she didn't marry my father, but I finally realized there's nothing I can do about it, which is why I try to forget.

"Oh," I said. "Well, tell her good-bye for me, will you?"

"Sure," Dad said, and pulled on his sport coat.

"What time is her plane?"

"It's a seven o'clock flight, so I'll grab a bite after I get back," he said. "You and Les will have to get your own dinner."

"Don't worry about us. We'll manage," I said.

Dad went out, and I watched his car back down the drive. Maybe it's a good thing I don't remember much about my mother, because if I did I suppose I'd resent Miss Summers and the way Dad loves her. I only remember a little bit, and even that gets all mixed up with memories of Aunt Sally, who took care of us for a while after the leukemia won and Mom died. Now all I want is for Dad to be happy.

I tried to think what I should have for dinner. Crackers and peanut butter? Shredded wheat?

"Hey, Les," I called when my brother came in. "Any ideas for dinner? Dad's taking Sylvia to the airport." Lester's working on a graduate degree in philosophy at the University of Maryland. He's also a part-time clerk at a shoe store, but I don't get discounts on anything.

"I'm taking Eva to dinner," he said, yanking off his T-shirt and racing upstairs to shower. "You're on your own, kid."

Well, great! I thought. *Just great!* Crackers and peanut butter it was, then. Maybe I should invite Patrick over for dinner. *That* would show them! And then I thought, why not?

I picked up the phone and dialed his number. "Patrick, you want to come over for dinner? I'm going solo tonight, and thought maybe we could make something."

"Like what? Pizza?" he asked.

Actually, I hadn't the foggiest idea. "I don't know," I said. "Whatever you want."

"I'd better check with Mom, see if she's made any-thing special," he said. And then he was back on the line. "We're having leftovers," he said. "I'll be there."

While he had been asking his mom, I'd walked into the kitchen with the phone and was staring inside our refrigerator. Half a grapefruit, a slice of meat loaf, and a bowl of chickpeas. A couple of tomatoes, half an onion . . . Was I insane?

My face! My hair! My teeth! I charged upstairs like a stampeding cow, colliding in the hallway with Lester, and changed my shirt. I was just brushing my teeth when the doorbell rang. Patrick always comes over on his bike, and I should have known he'd be here in two minutes.

"Hi," he said at the door. "What's for dinner?"

How do you say *nothing* and make it sound appetizing?

"Uh . . . ," I said. "Maybe I should take you out. I thought we could make supper together, but there's absolutely nothing in the fridge."

Upstairs I could hear Lester racing around, getting ready for his date with Eva, whom I'd never met. I don't think Dad had, either.

"Where *is* everyone?" Patrick asked.

"Dad's taking Miss Summers to the plane, and Lester's going out with his new girlfriend," I told him. "In a moment of madness I invited you over for dinner, and there's nothing to eat. C'mon. I'll treat you to a Big Mac."

"Hold on," said Patrick. "I had a hamburger for lunch. Let's take a look."

I'm not supposed to have boys in when no one else is home, but I'd be starting high school in September, and what could be more wholesome than eating dinner with a guy? Besides, I'd been deserted, and if both Dad and Lester were having company for dinner, so could I.

Patrick followed me out to the kitchen, and I sat on the table in my khaki shorts and yellow tank and watched. He moved stuff around and opened all the vegetable bins, and every so often he'd say, "Aha!" or, "Um hmm." Then he started taking stuff out—eggs, a tomato, cheese, butter . . .

"Have any potatoes?" he asked.

I looked in the bin where we keep potatoes and found one.

"Onions?" he asked.

I got him half an onion.

"Excellent," he said, and began slicing it thin.

I didn't have to do a thing. I just sat cross-legged on the table and watched Patrick making dinner, sautéing slices of onion in butter until the edges began to curl, then adding the potatoes and a little water and stirring them around.

Patrick's a couple of months younger than I am, but almost five inches taller. He's slim and strong and smart and funny and totally competent in whatever he does. I think it has something to do with the fact that his dad works for the state department, and they've lived in three or four different countries, so he's seen a lot of the world. He gets along with all kinds of people, and he's got self-confidence. We took a gourmet cooking class together in school last year, and he got a lot more out of it than I did.

I like him—I really do. There are times I think I'm crazy about him. But I always wonder what he sees in me. Why *me*? It's hard for me to imagine Patrick needing anyone, but here he was, in our kitchen, making dinner for *me*.

"Patrick," I said as he added tomatoes, then the egg mixture. "What do you like about me?"

He didn't even glance over. He was concentrating on sprinkling diced cheese on top of the eggs. "You're practical," he said.

Practical? That was my best quality? Men were going to sigh and pant and yearn for me because I was *practical*?

"What?" I bleated.

"What I mean is, you're not on a fast track, like Pamela, or stuck in reverse, like Elizabeth."

Fast track? Reverse? What were we, *cars*? Pamela was a sports car, maybe, and Elizabeth a station wagon, and I was—what—a practical little Honda? A family sedan?

"Also, you look good . . . ," Patrick continued.

"I look good? Like a cupcake, you mean? Patrick, I'm not a car, I'm not edible, I'm—"

"Will you let me finish?" he said. "Get some plates."

I opened the cupboard.

"I like your hair," he continued. "I like your feet. I like your shoulders and the way you smile. Especially your smile. Yeah. That's what I like about you, Alice. Your green eyes and your smile, okay? How'd I do?"

"Better," I said. I stood holding the plates while Patrick gently lifted the puffy egg mixture away from the sides of the pan, divided it into two portions, and put one on each plate.

"You got any bread to go with this? Any French or Italian?"

"Some sourdough, maybe."

"Perfect," he said, and we sat down to eat. In the space of fifteen or so minutes, Patrick had put together a tasty meal, and all I'd done was set the table. And then he said, "But you know what I like most about you?"

"My sexy body? My throaty laugh?"

"You're not phony," he said, and the way he said it, I knew he was serious. "That's something I can't stand in a girl. When a girl tries to act like somebody else or look like somebody else, or dresses wild just to be different, I always wonder why she's trying so hard."

That was even better than a throaty laugh.

The supper was really good.

"Maybe you should be a chef," I said, and when

he grunted, I asked, "How's the landscaping going?"

"Everything hurts," he said. "My shoulders, my back, my arms, my thighs. . . . It's good for me, though. I might even get a tan by the end of summer. Mostly I just burn. When do you start at the hospital?"

"Orientation's next week. Gwen and I are going together. I just hope I don't get assigned to bedpans," I told him.

Lester came galloping downstairs and stuck his head in the kitchen. "If Eva calls, tell her I'm on my way," he said. "Hi, Patrick. How's it going?"

"Good," said Patrick.

After the door closed, Patrick looked across the table at me and grinned. "Well!" he said.

I guess that's why parents don't want you to be alone in the house with a boy. That "well" could mean anything at all.

"So what do you want to do?" I asked. "Blackjack? Gin? Spit? Put on some CDs?"

"Spit," said Patrick.

We went into the living room, and while I got the cards, Patrick looked over our CD collection. It felt better being alone in the house with Patrick with music playing than sitting there listening to my stomach digest our dinner. I sat on the floor by our huge coffee table, and Patrick sat on the sofa.

We'd only played one game when we heard a car

drive up. A door slammed, then another. There were footsteps and voices on the porch, and Lester came inside with one of the most beautiful women I'd ever seen.

"Just a pit stop," Lester said. "Eva, this is my sister, Alice, and her friend Patrick. Guys, this is Eva Mecuri. Sit down, Eva. I'll just be a minute."

I couldn't understand why Lester would come all the way home to use the bathroom, but at that moment I was focusing on the tall, ultraslim woman walking across the room. Her skin was pale and creamy, her dark eyes almond shaped, and her black hair was cut in a short bob. Her dress was black, translucent layer on layer, with short sleeves and a neckline cut into a low V. She wore black stockings with black sling-back heels.

Eva's eyebrows were beautifully arched, the mascara on her lashes elegantly applied, the blush on her cheekbones perfectly placed, and her red, red lipstick outlined a heart-shaped mouth. I couldn't imagine where Lester had met her, but what mattered was that she was here in our house and, compared to her, I felt like a banana peel at the bottom of the garbage pail. I tugged at my shorts so they weren't so wrinkled looking and straightened my tank top.

"Hi," I said.

"Hello, Alice. Hi, Patrick," the gorgeous thing

said, and took a seat next to the sofa, crossing her silky legs. You couldn't see anything under her short dress, so I suppose all her underwear was black, too.

"School's out, I guess?" she said.

"Yeah, good old summertime," said Patrick, reshuffling the cards.

"What grade will you be going into?" Eva asked.

"We're starting high school," I told her.

"Ninth," Patrick added.

"Wonderful," said Eva, glancing at her watch and then at the stairs.

Patrick dealt the cards, but I didn't pick mine up. I just wanted to drink in Eva Mecuri with my eyes, studying her colors, her curves—the careless way she tossed her head and ran one hand through her jet-black hair.

I was relieved, though, when Lester came back down, even though I hadn't heard the toilet flush.

"Ready," he said, and then I noticed he'd changed his tie.

Eva rose from her chair and gave a tinkly little laugh. "Darling, it's *crooked!*" she said. "Here, let me fix it." And she fussed around with his shirt collar. "Now," she said, "you're presentable."

"Bye again," Lester said.

"It was nice to meet you, Alice. You, too, Peter," the vision in black said.

"Patrick," said Patrick.

The door closed behind them, and Patrick and I looked at each other.

"He came all the way back home just to change his tie?" I exclaimed.

"Bet she made him," said Patrick.

I went to the window to watch Eva get in the car. "Where do you suppose he met her?" I said.

"Shopping at Saks, maybe?" said Patrick. We played a few more games, and then he pulled me up beside him. He put his arm around me and said, "Your dad going to pop out of the closet about now?"

I think we were both remembering how Dad had clicked on the porch light a few weeks before when we were kissing passionately on the swing. I wondered if Les and Eva kissed passionately. I couldn't imagine her messing up her dress or her hair or makeup. I couldn't even imagine her without makeup.

But right at that moment Patrick was kissing me, and I realized that there is a lot of difference between kissing outside in the dark and kissing indoors with a light on. I mean, anybody could have seen. *We* could see, that was the problem. All I had to do was open my eyes to see whether Patrick kissed with his eyes open or closed, so I looked and, oh, m'gosh, *Patrick* was looking.

I jerked away from him.

"You're staring at me!" I said.

"*You* were staring at *me!*" He laughed. He glanced around the room. "Actually, I can't help thinking that your dad has the place booby-trapped."

I grinned. "He'd have surveillance cameras around if he could," I told him.

Patrick put his arm around me again, but this time he whispered into my hair, "You got any ice cream?"

I was almost glad, because I was uncomfortable kissing with the light on, but if we turned it off, Dad might come home.

"Almond mocha fudge?" I asked.

"That'll do," said Patrick.

We went back out in the kitchen, and I found a jar of milk chocolate topping, which Patrick insisted on heating before we poured it over the ice cream.

"Why settle for ordinary if you can have gourmet?" he said.

I was halfway through mine when I remembered that Pamela and Elizabeth and I had sworn off ice cream for the summer. I ate it, anyway, and it was delicious. I was just rinsing the dish afterward when Dad came in. He seemed surprised to find Patrick there and Lester out, but I could tell he was feeling pretty good just by the way his eyes crinkled at the corners when he smiled.

"You want an ice-cream sundae, Dad?" I offered. "Patrick made dinner for me, and we're having dessert."

He took off his sport coat and draped it over the back of a chair, then opened the refrigerator. "No, I think I'll just have an apple," he said, rummaging through the fruit bin. "Maybe a sandwich later. How are things going, Patrick?"

"Pretty good," Patrick told him. "I have to get up every morning at the crack of dawn, but other than that, I like to work outside."

"Makes a nice change from school," said Dad.

He took his apple into the living room, and Patrick said, "Well, I'd better get home. Landscaper wants me there by six-thirty tomorrow. We're loading a truck and doing some planting up near Frederick."

"Okay," I told him, and walked him out on the porch, where he kissed me in the dark. Better. Definitely better.

"Yep," he said, pulling away after a moment. "You really look good, cupcake." Then he kissed me again, his lips hard against my mouth, his tongue pushing against my teeth. I felt a *zing* go through me, and wondered what would happen if I ever *was* in the house alone with Patrick and we knew for sure Dad wouldn't be there.

At the end of the kiss, Patrick held my face in his hands and said, "Why settle for ordinary when you can have gourmet?"

I smiled at him, and then he was going down the steps to his bike.

After he'd gone, I went back inside to find Dad sitting contentedly on the couch, eating his apple. He looked very pleased with himself. Maybe Miss Summers didn't leave after all! I thought. Maybe she had started down the ramp to the plane, and suddenly turned around and thrown herself in his arms! Maybe Dad had proposed on the spot and she'd accepted, and the whole terminal had burst into applause.

"Did . . . did Miss Summers get off okay?" I asked.

"Oh, yes," said Dad. "Plane was right on time."

I waited, and when he didn't offer any more, I grinned at him. "It must have been a long goodbye. I thought you'd be back before this."

"Oh, I stopped at the United counter and bought my ticket for England. I'll be visiting her, you know, the last two weeks of August."

So many things were going through my mind at once that it was like opening the dryer door while the clothes inside were still spinning and trying to find your socks. He was really going to do it! Dad and Miss Summers would be alone together for two whole weeks this summer! Then the second thought: Les and I would be here by ourselves for two whole weeks while Dad was away.

"That's . . . that's wonderful, Dad!" I said. I gathered up the cards from the coffee table and started to put them away.

"Les is out?" Dad asked.

"Yeah, he and Eva. He stopped by the house to change his tie. She must not have liked it."

"What's she like?"

I thought. "Sort of the Mata Hari type."

"Mata Hari!" Dad exclaimed. "Where did you pick that up? What do you know about *her?*"

I hadn't the slightest idea. I think it was a name I'd heard him use. "You mean she's a real person?"

"She was a spy back in World War I. She was supposed to have seduced our soldiers and demoralized the troops. No . . . wait a minute. Maybe that was Tokyo Rose in World War II."

"Whatever," I said. As far as I was concerned, either one fit Eva all right. I started for the dining room to put the cards back in the drawer when Dad said, "I thought we had a rule about Patrick, Al."

I turned. "About *Patrick?* Just Patrick?"

"About any boy in the house when no one else is home."

"Dad, all we did was make dinner and play cards and eat some ice cream," I said. *And kiss,* I should have added, but didn't.

"Al," he said, "I was fourteen once. And I know how exciting and tempting it is to be alone with someone you find attractive. The rule still stands, even though you're entering high school. *Especially* now that you're entering high school. And if you don't think you can stick to it while I'm away in August, I could ask your aunt Sally to fly out from Chicago and—"

"Never mind," I said. "I get the point."

3

Volunteer

Gwen and I agreed to meet in the lobby of the hospital on Monday at nine in the morning and apply as volunteers. We both arrived early, so we sat on a couch together and tried to figure what color of uniform would look best on us. She's got brown skin and black hair; I'm a strawberry blonde, and my skin is pale. The only color we could come up with that suited us both was yellow.

It wasn't until we met our supervisor and she gave us the applications that I realized how small my world really was:

Job experience: Three hours a week for my dad.
Languages spoken: English only.
Hobbies and skills: Junior High Camera Club . . .
 Scrubbing the porch?
Education: Eighth grade, beginning ninth.
Why do you want to be a volunteer?

I thought about that last question. *To get experience*, I wrote. It was the only thing I could think of, and I did need different kinds of experiences. A more honest answer would probably have been, *So I can wear a uniform*. If I wore a uniform, I'd feel more important. And if I *felt* important, maybe I was.

Gwen and I looked at each other.

"I don't guess we look all that great on paper," she said.

"Everybody has to start somewhere," I told her.

We turned to the next page of the application and discovered that the uniform consisted of a jacket. No striped pinafores. No pink aprons. No official-looking caps or dresses.

It was when we read the volunteer agreement that we discovered just what would be required of us. We had to agree to keep all information about patients confidential; volunteer at least one four-hour day per week; be punctual; wear our ID badges each time; get a tuberculosis skin test, a chest X ray, and provide our own transportation.

In other words, we didn't get brownie points for being volunteers. Nobody was coming to pick us up; we had to be punctual, discreet, and work without pay. The giving would be all on our part. Could we do it?

Gwen signed without hesitating a minute. I

signed my name. We both had to take the forms home for a parent's signature. Then we went in to talk with the supervisor.

"There are many things you can do here," she told us, "but we'll probably start you out doing a little of everything. You can help deliver mail and flowers to patients' rooms. You can stock shelves in the gift shop and replace magazines in the waiting rooms. We need volunteers to change beds in physical therapy, to move patients in wheelchairs to cars, and of course there's a right way to do all of this, and we'll make sure you know how."

We watched a short training film with other volunteers and then we had to sign up for certain days of the week. Gwen and I had already talked it over and decided on Monday, Wednesday, and Friday mornings from nine to one, because we wanted it to seem like a real job. That gave us afternoons off, of course, to swim or whatever.

I think both Gwen and I were more confused than helpful the first day. Just getting around the hospital was a headache, learning which floors held the cardiac unit, intensive care, maternity, orthopedic, oncology (cancer), psychiatric, pediatric—the list went on and on. Then there were the visitors' elevators and the emergency elevator, freight elevators . . . staff rooms, nuclear medicine rooms . . .

"Maybe this will get us in shape for high school," Gwen said. "All those corridors, all those rooms . . ."

We didn't see much of each other the rest of the day, because we were each assigned to another volunteer who showed us how to put the brakes on a wheelchair before a patient sat down, how to enter a patient's room without intruding, what we could say to patients and what we couldn't.

"Why did we ever pick *mornings!*" Gwen moaned as we fell into a seat on the bus going home and the door closed behind us. "I'm not even awake till ten o'clock."

"So we'd have our afternoons off," I reminded her.

"I'd rather sleep," Gwen said, drawing her feet up on the seat and leaning her head on my shoulder.

On Wednesday, though, when I met Gwen on the bus, we both felt more ready. We were wearing the jackets they'd given us the first day—coral-colored things that looked better on Gwen than on me—with our IDs attached to the pockets, and when we walked through the swinging doors of the hospital, we felt as though we belonged.

My job for the first hour was to greet people at the admitting desk, check their names off on a list of patients to be admitted, jot down their time of arrival, and give them a clipboard with a form to fill out. If they had any questions I couldn't answer, I referred them to an older volunteer.

When the first four patients had signed in and we were waiting for more, the gray-haired woman behind the desk said to me, "What we have to remember, Alice, is that these aren't like customers in a restaurant. They're not here because they want to be, and they know they're not going to enjoy it. Every one of them has an ache or a pain somewhere. Some are seriously ill, and probably all of them are a little frightened. People who are worried don't always listen as well or follow instructions. They may be short-tempered, even rude. We have to allow for that."

I hadn't really thought of patients that way.

"They say," the volunteer continued, "that the only really happy ward in a hospital is maternity, where most of the women *are* there because they want to be. Because pregnancy is a natural, positive process."

Something else I hadn't thought of.

Gwen and I met in the cafeteria at one. We decided we could afford to treat ourselves to a burger after a four-hour stint as a volunteer, and it gave us a chance to unwind before we caught the bus home.

"What did they have you doing?" I asked her.

"Stocking shelves in the gift shop," she said. "I'd

rather work with patients. This was too much like working at the mall."

We both, though, felt wiped out.

"Just tension," Dad told me that evening. "It's a new situation, and the people you're meeting are under stress, too. It's natural. It'll take a while."

He was right, because the third time we went—Friday—I knew just where to sign in, where to report, and I began to feel I was part of the team. Some of the people I'd already met said hello to me, and it felt good going around with my ID tag dangling from my jacket pocket. I'd tried a number of different jobs, but this time I got the one I liked most, taking mail and flowers around to the patients.

"Take a cart," my supervisor said. "The green plant goes to 207, and the yellow roses go to 510. The magazines go to the waiting room at maternity."

I put the plants and magazines on a cart and got on an elevator. A doctor smiled at me. "You've signed up for the summer?" he asked.

I nodded.

"How many days are you volunteering a week?"

"Three. Just the mornings," I told him.

"We're glad to have you," he said. "Welcome aboard."

It was a new kind of feeling, being needed. I

mean, I knew I was needed at home, and I think Elizabeth and Pamela and some of my other friends need me—some of the time, anyway. Patrick *acts* like he needs me, though I can't imagine why. But here in the hospital, I knew that if I didn't volunteer, all my jobs would fall to someone else who already had his hands full. It's nice to do something different for a change.

I delivered the green plant to room 207—the man was sleeping, so I just put it on his windowsill and went back out. Then I took the elevator to 510. I was getting more familiar with the different floors—where to find the nursing stations, how the rooms were numbered. Fifth floor, I remembered, was the cardiac unit.

In 510, one bed was empty, but there was a woman in the bed near the window. I couldn't tell if she was sleeping or not, but I knocked lightly on the door and went in just as she turned her face toward me. I stopped and stared.

"Why . . . Alice? Is it you?" the woman said, and I recognized my sixth-grade teacher, Mrs. Plotkin.

"Mrs. Plotkin!" I said. "I didn't know you were here!"

"Why, of course you didn't, my dear. How could you? I didn't know I was going to be here myself. We were out having dinner with friends the other day, and I had this little heart problem again.

Strange, isn't it, how one body part wears out before another." She smiled and put out her hand, grasping my arm and pulling me gently toward her. "Let me look at you, dear. My, haven't you gotten pretty, though! Not that you weren't before. How *are* you?"

I put her yellow roses on the windowsill and handed her the card. They were from some friends in Silver Spring. Then I sat down beside her bed. The training film had taught us that when a patient wants to talk and we can afford the time, we can sit down with them for a few minutes. We're not to give any medical advice, of course, and we're to keep the conversation on pleasant subjects, when possible, but most of all, we're to be good listeners. I didn't have to be told to be a good listener for my favorite teacher.

She was thinner now than she was three years ago, and her hair was a lot more gray. But she still had that kind smile on her face and in her eyes. I wanted to put my arms around her and hug her, but I didn't know if volunteers were supposed to do that.

"You're a volunteer in this hospital now? Isn't that wonderful!" she said. "How well you look! Tell me about your friends."

I tried to remember who else was in her sixth-grade class with me. Elizabeth, I think, had Mr.

Weber, but Pamela and Patrick were in my class. "Well, I'm friends with Pamela Jones," I said. I wondered whether I should tell her about Pamela's mom running off with a boyfriend, and decided against it. That subject was neither happy nor hopeful.

"Pamela Jones," Mrs. Plotkin mused. "Now, wasn't she the girl in the play who . . . ?" This time it was Mrs. Plotkin's turn to stop talking.

I smiled. "Yes, the girl in the starring role. The one whose hair I grabbed onstage."

We looked at each other and both started to laugh. She just kept looking at me and smiling. "My, how grown-up you seem, Alice. Who else might I remember?"

"Patrick Long?"

"Oh, yes, the red-haired boy."

"He's still my boyfriend," I said.

"Oh, my!" She smiled at me again. "So sophisticated, he was. I always liked Patrick."

"So did I," I told her.

A nurse came in just then. "Well, look who's awake," she said. "I came in fifteen minutes ago, but you were sleeping so soundly, I decided to leave you be. But the doctor has you down for another test this morning."

Mrs. Plotkin wrinkled her nose at me. "Why, this is worse than school!" she said.

"I'll come back on Monday," I told her, standing up. "I volunteer three times a week."

"Well, if they're still keeping me here, dear, I'd like that," she said. "I love visiting with you."

The nurse smiled at me, and I said, "My favorite teacher."

She looked at Mrs. Plotkin. "Well, she's a pretty nice patient, too."

I went out in the hall to take the magazines on up to maternity, and realized I hadn't asked Mrs. Plotkin how *she* was doing. *I am so self-centered!* I told myself. There she was in the cardiac unit, and I chatter on about *my* friends, *my* job. Why didn't I ask her about herself?

When I met Gwen in the cafeteria for lunch, I told her what a dork I was with my teacher. She put one finger to her lips.

"What?" I said, looking around.

"We aren't supposed to do that," Gwen reminded me, rolling her eyes as she stuffed a French fry in her mouth.

"Do what?"

"Talk about patients. If you see a patient here you know, you're not supposed to tell anyone about it."

Three days as a volunteer, and I'd already broken one rule.

•   •   •

It proved even more difficult at dinner that evening, because the more I thought about Mrs. Plotkin in the cardiac unit, the more worried I became. What if she was really, really sick? I wondered if I should call her husband and find out just how sick she was. Maybe I shouldn't wait till Monday to go see her again. I sat staring at my plate, turning my pork chop over and over with my fork.

"You looking for bugs under there or something?" Lester asked.

I picked up my knife and cut off a piece. "I'm just worried about someone I saw in the hospital today," I said.

"Who was that?" asked Dad.

"I can't tell you."

"What do you mean you can't tell us?" asked Lester. "Who are you? The Secret Service?"

"I'm supposed to keep all information about patients confidential," I told them. "It's part of the agreement I signed."

"Well, then, I guess you'd better not say anything," said Dad.

I sighed. "I just hope she doesn't die."

Dad put down his fork. "Al, is this someone we know?"

I thought about it. They'd certainly heard me talk about her when I was in sixth grade, and Dad had met her at parent-teacher conferences.

"Yes," I said.

"Male or female?" asked Lester.

"Female," I said.

"Well, it can't be Janice Sherman, because she was at the store today," said Dad, referring to his assistant manager at the Melody Inn. "And it can't be Marilyn, because she was there too." Marilyn is Lester's ex-girlfriend. She works for Dad.

I realized that if I kept answering their questions, they'd eventually hit the jackpot, so I pressed my lips together.

"Eva?" asked Lester. "Was it *Eva?*"

And when I didn't speak, he asked, *"Crystal?"* (An ex-girlfriend who's married).

I thought about the agreement I'd signed, the volunteer's jacket with my ID clipped to the pocket, and the doctors and nurses who smiled at me in the elevator. I was part of a team.

"You can beat me and starve me and pull out my fingernails with red-hot pinchers, but I'll never tell," I said proudly. "But I can tell you one thing: Everyone loves her."

"The First Lady, obviously," said Lester. "Listen, Al, if it's Eva, rap once on the table. If it's Crystal, rap twice. If it's . . . "

I shook my head vigorously and put my hands beneath me in the chair.

Dad was getting impatient with me. "If you can't tell us, why did you even bring it up?" he said. "If it's a good customer of mine, I think I should know."

"I brought it up because I wondered if it was permissible to call a close relative of hers to find out how sick she really was," I told him. "I mean, if she died, and . . . "

"So how did *you* find out about this person?" asked Lester.

"I didn't even know she was there! I was taking some flowers up to 510 and when I walked in, there she was!" I said.

Lester got up from the table, went down the hall, and looked up a number in the phone book. Then he brought the phone back to the kitchen doorway and pressed some numbers on the handset.

"Patient information, please," he said. And a moment later, "Can you please tell me how the patient in 510 is doing?" he asked, and held the receiver out away from his ear so we could hear.

"Sara Plotkin? Her condition is fair, and she's resting comfortably," came the reply.

"Thank you," Lester said, and hung up.

"You shouldn't have done that," I told him.

"Well, you shouldn't have brought it up," said Lester. "I was afraid it might be Eva."

Dad looked over at me. "Mrs. Plotkin? Your sixth-grade teacher?"

"Yes."

"It's good that you're following the rules, Al, but I don't think the hospital would mind if you'd simply mentioned your former teacher to your family. What they don't want is you broadcasting a patient's personal medical problems to the world. Anyway, she appears to be out of danger."

"I guess so," I told him.

But after I went to bed that night, I thought how the report *might* have said that her condition was *excellent*. It could even have said *good*. I would have settled for *satisfactory*. But it didn't. It said *fair,* which was one step up from *poor*. I knew that my first stop on Monday would be to room 510 to see if she was still there.

4

Quiz

Since Pamela's mom moved to Colorado with her boyfriend, things have been pretty grim over at Pamela's place. Elizabeth and I don't go there much. When the three of us want an overnight, we come either to my house or Elizabeth's. Lester always says to let him know when the gaggle of witches is gathering, because our cackling drives him nuts. So I told him they were coming over Saturday night, and he made plans to play baseball at the park with some of his buddies.

When Elizabeth and Pamela arrived, though, he was still waiting for a couple of his friends to come by. He and Dad were sitting at the dining room table looking over the grant Lester had received from the University of Maryland for his graduate studies, figuring how much more they'd have to come up with to pay tuition in the fall.

"You've got *YM!*" I cried when Pamela came in,

seeing one of our favorite magazines. Elizabeth was carrying *Teen* and *Seventeen,* too. I opened some sodas, and the three of us hunkered down on the couch to look them over—Pamela in the middle, and Elizabeth and I on either side.

"Now *that,*" said Elizabeth, pointing to a bone-thin girl in a slip dress on the inside cover, "is how I want to look."

"What is she? A poster child for starvation?" I said.

"She's modeling a dress," Elizabeth told me.

"Looks like an ad for TB," said Pamela. "She doesn't have any curves! She's all angles!"

"I think she's gorgeous," said Elizabeth, and turned the page.

There are always more ads than articles in these magazines, and when it's a magazine for girls, half the ads are for zit cream, it seems. There was a double-page ad for earrings, titled "Ear Power," but Elizabeth dismissed it with a wave of her hand. "None of those earrings are any fun," she said. Pamela liked a photo spread on body piercing, though. "That is so cool!" she said. "I want my navel pierced, and I want two more holes in each earlobe."

"Not a nose ring, though," said Elizabeth. "Those are really gross. Especially when you get a cold." We agreed.

The problem with looking at magazines with Pamela and Elizabeth is that they like to look at articles about clothes and hair and makeup and stuff. I like the quizzes. We all do, really.

"Wait," I said, flipping back a few pages. "I saw a quiz."

"'Do You Have Bedroom Eyes?'" Pamela read aloud, and we all shrieked. "Get a pencil," she said. "We've got to take this one."

Pamela read the questions aloud, all three of us answered, and Elizabeth tallied our scores.

"Question one," said Pamela. "'Do you flirt with your eyes or your smile?'"

"Eyes," said Pamela.

"Smile," I said.

"Smile," said Elizabeth.

"No, you don't, Elizabeth, you flirt with your eyes," Pamela told her. "I've seen you." She read the next question: "'Using your thumb as a measure, are your eyes a thumb-length apart, three-quarters of a thumb-length apart, or half a thumb length apart?'"

We measured and judged each other. Elizabeth was the only one whose eyes were a thumb-length apart, so only she had authentic bedroom eyes. Pamela and I both measure three-quarters of a thumb length. But if your eyes are close together, don't despair, the quiz said. By concentrating your eye liner at the outer edges of your eyes, you will create the illusion of widely spaced eyes. Never bring your eye liner all the way to the inner corners of your eyes unless, like Jackie Kennedy, you have unbelievably widely spaced eyes.

"Wow, Elizabeth, you're so lucky!" said Pamela.

Who decides these things? I wondered. "Quiz by Marcia Kent." Who the heck was Marcia Kent? How come *she* got to decide who had bedroom eyes and who didn't? And did I really want bedroom eyes in the first place? If I become a psychiatrist, like I think I want to be, will they help me there?

"Next," said Pamela. "'Do your eyes, lids included, most resemble almonds, hazelnuts, or Brazil nuts?'" We whooped with laughter.

"This is really dumb," I said, wrestling the magazine away from Pamela. "Let's find another one." We flipped past a picture of a bunch of guys playing touch football in their swim trunks.

"Isn't he *hot?*" Pamela squealed, pointing to a guy with washboard abs.

"There's one!" said Elizabeth, spotting another quiz as I turned. "Are You a Tease?" it asked.

"Pamela, this one's for you," I told her, and read the first question. "'When wearing a shirt, do you usually A) button it to the top? B) leave the top unbuttoned? C) leave the second button open, too? D) leave as much open as possible?'"

"Now *this* one is stupid!" Elizabeth declared.

"A for Elizabeth, D for Pamela," I said, and Elizabeth reached around and poked me.

One of Lester's friends knocked at the door just then, and Lester left the dining room and went out in the hallway to let him in. His name was Jack Grafton, and he was probably one of the shyest guys I'd ever seen. Most of Lester's guy friends are like Les, sort of extroverted and funny, but Jack's almost a year younger, and the few times I've spoken to him, he seems terribly uncomfortable. He's cute—real blond with a square face and just a touch of beard neatly rimming his jaw. I could tell that Elizabeth and Pamela were studying him over the top of the magazine.

"Bud coming?" Jack asked Lester.

"Yeah. He'll be here in a little while—the others will be at the park," Les told him. "Let me go up and change my shirt. Be with you in a moment. Sit down."

Jack glanced in at us, then turned and looked beseechingly after Lester as he disappeared up the stairs. Finally he walked over to a chair in the living room and sat down, looking hopefully out the window. His face was a faint shade of pink.

Pamela nudged me. I think this was the first

time Jack had been in a room with me without Lester, and now he had Elizabeth and Pamela to deal with, too.

"Uh, Pamela . . . Elizabeth . . . this is Jack Grafton," I said.

"Hi, Jack," said Elizabeth.

"Hi, Grafton," said Pamela.

Jack's face grew pinker still, and he glanced over at us as though seeing us for the first time. "Hi," he said, and looked toward the window again.

Pamela gave a muffled giggle. "We're taking a quiz," she told Jack. "Want to take it with us?"

I poked her, but it didn't make any difference.

Jack forced a smile. "I'm not very good at quizzes," he said.

Then Elizabeth got in the act. "Oh, there aren't any right or wrong answers," she said. "It's just to see whether or not you're a tease."

I exchanged looks with Elizabeth. Jack didn't answer.

Pamela giggled again. "Question one," she said. "'When wearing a shirt, do you usually A) button it to the top? B) leave the top unbuttoned? C) leave the second button open, too? D) leave as much open as possible?'"

Jack seemed to be trying to figure out if we were serious or not. He shrugged. "I don't wear those kinds of shirts much," he said.

I couldn't help myself. "Give him B, Pamela," I said. "You keeping score, Elizabeth?"

"Yeah. That gives you two points, Jack," Elizabeth said.

"Question two," said Pamela. "'Do you typically kiss with your mouth open or closed?'"

Jack's face grew as pink as cotton candy. "That's pretty personal," he said.

"Open!" Elizabeth and I said together.

"We'll give Jack three points," said Pamela. "Okay. Next question. 'When wearing jeans, do you flaunt your butt?'" All three of us broke into giggles. Jack looked so pained that I should have stopped Pamela right there. If he had been closer to our age, I might have felt sorry for him, but at nineteen or twenty, I figured he should be over this by now. A car drove up, and Jack jerked around, hoping it was the third baseman, but then the car went on by.

"Maybe we should try him on another quiz, Pamela," I said. "Let's see if he has bedroom eyes."

"Oh, yes! Definitely!" said Elizabeth.

Lester came down just then, and Jack practically leaped out of the chair, wanting to get away. But his face fell when Les came in and sat down. "Bud said he might be a little late," he told Jack. "Should have told him to meet us at the park." Jack sat back down, but he looked so miserable that Lester figured out we'd been teasing him.

"What no-brain quiz are you girls taking?" he asked.

Elizabeth was already flipping through the second magazine. "Here's an article for you, Lester," she said. "'Ten Things Guys Can't Understand About Gals.'"

"Ha! I could name you twenty," said Lester. "I don't need a quiz for that. For starters, how come girls are always taking quizzes? Do you understand that, Jack?"

Jack shook his head.

I looked at Pamela and Elizabeth. "I don't know. How come we *do* take quizzes?"

"We learn about ourselves this way," said Elizabeth, making a guess.

"You have to take a quiz to figure out who you are?" Lester said.

"We compare ourselves with other girls to see how we're different," I told him.

"You're different, all right," said Lester. "Weird, weirder, and weirdest."

Now it was Jack's turn to laugh.

"So what don't you understand about women, Lester?" Pamela asked flirtatiously. She and Elizabeth have had a crush on Lester since the day we moved in, I think.

Lester thought about it a moment. "The way

you obsess about the way you look," he said. "When do you ever hear a guy say, 'I wonder if these pants make me look fat?' or, 'Does this go okay with my hair?' Guys don't talk that way, do we, Jack?"

"No. Sure don't," Jack said, looking a lot more comfortable now that Lester was in the room.

"Here's another one," said Lester. "Whenever girls go to a restaurant with a bunch of people, if one goes to the rest room, they all get up and go. You ever notice that? Girls go to the bathroom in gangs. They all get the urge at the same time? Explain that to me."

Pamela, Elizabeth, and I looked at each other.

"We do?" I asked.

"Yeah, he's right," said Elizabeth. "We *do* that."

"Why?" I wondered.

"So we can talk about the guys," Pamela suggested.

"Right!" I looked at Jack and Lester. "We go off together to talk about the guys. Half the time we don't even use the facilities. We just gather there at the sink and comb our hair and talk."

"Amazing," said Lester. "Absolutely amazing."

A door slammed out front.

"There's Bud!" Jack said, leaping to his feet.

"Good-byyyeee, Jack!" cooed Pamela. "Maybe I'll call you sometime."

Jack was already out the door.

"Good-bye, Les," called Elizabeth.

"Good-bye, witches. Have a good cackle," Lester called.

When they were gone, Elizabeth said, "How come girls are attracted to older guys like that?"

"I'm attracted to Patrick, and he's a couple months younger than I am," I reminded her.

"Yeah, but in general. That would make a good quiz for one of these magazines," said Elizabeth. "We ought to suggest it."

"So let's write one," I said.

Dad was still trying to work at the dining room table, which he was using for a desk, so we trooped up to my room and sprawled out on my bed with a notebook. My bedroom is decorated in a sort of jungle motif—a lion-print spread, a koala bear pillow, and a huge rubber plant in one corner.

"What'll we call our quiz?" asked Pamela.

"What about 'Your Fave Fella?'" suggested Elizabeth. "'If you could choose the ideal guy, he would be: A) older than you, B) younger, C) about the same age, D) doesn't matter?'"

I grinned and wrote it down. "Number two," I said. "Older guys are A) more fun; B) more dangerous; C)—"

"More boring?" said Pamela.

"No, conceited," said Elizabeth. "And D) more

bald." We laughed. "Oh, this is good!" she went on. "Now . . . three: Your ideal date would own A) a guitar; B) A bike; C) A dog—"

"A dog? Gimme a break!" said Pamela.

"That's important, Pamela! You can tell a lot about a guy by how he treats a pet," I told her.

"And D)," Elizabeth finished, "a car."

I had another idea. "Here's one: Your fave fella drinks A) champagne; B) beer; C) root beer; D)—"

"Milk," finished Elizabeth. We howled.

"You like your fave fella best in A) a suit; B) a sweat suit . . ." Pamela began.

"Swim suit," added Elizabeth.

"His birthday suit," I finished. We rolled over on our backs and shrieked.

Dad knocked on the door of my room. He was wearing a pair of plaid shorts and an old T-shirt from the Melody Inn with the words HAPPY BIRTH-DAY, BEETHOVEN on the front. He had sandals on his feet, and though he's sort of pudgy around the middle, he's got the skinniest legs and the knob-biest knees you ever saw.

"Is this the usual hysteria, or somebody here need a doctor?" he asked.

We stared at my dad a moment and then we broke into laughter again. We just couldn't help ourselves. Dad smiled and shrugged and closed the door.

Pamela was laughing so hard, she had tears in her eyes. "I'll take the younger guys," she said.

"Even the milk drinkers," said Elizabeth.

"Without plaid shorts," I added.

"Definitely without shorts. No shorts at all," said Pamela.

When Patrick called that night, I asked if he and the guys ever took quizzes.

"What do you mean?"

"In magazines. Just for fun," I told him.

"Why would we want to do that?" he asked. "We get enough at school."

Like they say, women are from Venus, men from Mars.

5

Saving Lester

When I went to the hospital on Monday, I found out that Mrs. Plotkin had been discharged. I was relieved that things turned out okay, but sorry I couldn't drop in her room again to talk. When I got home that day, however, I got news of another kind. Lester was going on a weeklong trip to the Rockies with one of his guy friends, Gary.

Seems that Gary had racked up two tickets to Colorado on his frequent-flier miles—Gary was a technician with an audiovisual company—and this was a chance Lester might never get again. They'd known each other for three years, and of all the friends Gary could have picked to go to the Rockies with him, it was Lester.

"A good way to spend the Fourth of July," Dad said at dinner after Lester had told us. "But what about those two summer classes you're taking? And your job at the shoe store? Will they let you off?"

"I made a deal with the manager. I'll be working Labor Day weekend when everyone else wants to be at the beach, and also Thanksgiving weekend. And I'll only miss one session of classes. I'm working ahead so I can afford the time."

"Great!" said Dad. "What all do you guys plan on doing?"

"We're staying at Estes Park and want to do some hiking," Lester told us. "Gary wants to climb Longs Peak. I told him I'm up for it."

I stopped chewing. Dad was going to England to visit Miss Summers, and Les was going to climb a peak? I was definitely turning into Elizabeth, but I suddenly wondered what would happen to me if Dad's plane crashed and Lester fell off the mountain. Or maybe I was really thinking how come Dad got to go to England and Les to Colorado and I wasn't going anywhere.

I could feel tears springing to my eyes, and I hate that, so I tried to get angry, instead. "Well, that's just great!" I said. "Have a good time in England, Dad. Have a marvelous climb up Longs Peak, Lester. I'll just slog away the summer as a hospital volunteer. Thanks for thinking of me."

Dad put down his fork. Les had just lifted his glass to his lips, but he paused and stared at me over the rim.

"Something eating you, Al?" asked Dad. "I don't

remember either Lester or I complaining last year when you and Elizabeth and Pamela took that trip to Chicago on Amtrak. As I recall, you had a fairly good time."

A tear escaped in spite of myself. "But what . . . what if . . . if something happens to you guys?" I whispered.

"Hey, we're not leaving you here alone!" Dad said. "Lester's going next week, and I'm going in August. Something could happen to me just crossing Georgia Avenue, but you don't worry about that, do you?"

I still didn't want Lester to go. I wanted Dad to have a good time because I wanted Miss Summers to marry him, but I couldn't think of a good reason for Lester to risk his neck in Colorado when he could be here introducing me to his cute friends.

"What about Eva?" I asked, pulling out all the stops.

"What about her?"

"What does she think of you being gone for a whole week?"

"It so happens that Eva will be in New York at a sales conference for three of those days, so I doubt I'll be missed," Lester told me.

I was still sniffling. "What does she sell?"

"Perfumes and cosmetics. She's a representative for Revlon or Estée Lauder or one of those companies."

That figured. Eva's makeup looked to me as though it took an hour to apply. But I was horrified to discover *two* tears rolling down my cheeks. What was *wrong* with me?

"Well, I don't want you to go," I sobbed, and felt five years old. It was as though someone else had set my emotional thermostat and I didn't have a thing to say about it.

"Deal with it, Al," said Lester.

"You'll cope," said Dad.

I sure couldn't expect any sympathy there. Not even from Patrick, I found out later. When he came over that night, I told him I was worried about Lester climbing Longs Peak.

"Why?" asked Patrick.

"Why do you think? Because he might fall."

"But how will he know if he can do it or not if he doesn't try?" Patrick said.

"The point is, this is not something he *has* to do, Patrick! And if he falls off and kills himself, he'll have no life at all!"

Patrick only shrugged. "But if he makes it, he can always say, 'I climbed Longs Peak.'"

We don't even speak the same language.

Two days before Lester was to leave for the Rockies, he picked up Eva at whatever department store she was training clerks, and brought her to our house to change into the tennis outfit she'd brought along. They were going to play a few games, then come back here to shower and change and go out for dinner.

"Eva, this is my dad," Lester said. "Dad, Eva Mecuri."

I was sitting cross-legged in my beanbag chair in one corner of the living room reading a novel called *Ice*, hoping, maybe, it would cool me off.

"How nice to meet you," Dad said, getting up from the couch where he'd been sorting the mail.

"It's a pleasure," said Eva, extending her hand. She was wearing a white linen two-piece dress, white stockings, and white shoes. Her black hair had been pulled away from her face and held in place in back with a large black ribbon. Her perfectly shaped brows and perfectly shaped lips and perfectly outlined eyes had that painted-on look. "And how are you, Alice?" she asked, turning to me.

"Fine," I told her. Since we'd already been introduced, I didn't feel it was necessary to stand up. Dad hates my beanbag chair and says it doesn't go with any of the other furniture in our living room, but I've had it since I was four and I sort of think of that little space in the living room as my comfort corner, the way you keep a dog's bed behind the couch or something. I heard Aunt Sally tell

Uncle Milt once that I'd got that beanbag chair for Christmas the year my mother died, and that I was probably clinging to it as a "lap substitute." Maybe that's why I want to be a psychiatrist.

"Al," said Lester, "would you let Eva use your room to change?"

"Sure," I said, and suddenly remembered the socks and underwear that were strewn all over the place. "I'll take you up," I said, leaping to my feet.

I could smell Eva's perfume as she came up the stairs behind me, and I wondered what happens when perfume collides with the smell of sweaty socks. What happened was, she winced. I turned just in time to see her eyebrows come together over the bridge of her nose. I kicked a pair of underpants under my bed, and grabbed a bra that was hanging over a chair. A box of Kotex was perched right there on my dresser, as though it were the centerpiece, and I grabbed it and tried to tuck it under my arm as I headed for half a cheese sandwich that had been molding on my windowsill for a week.

"Would you have a hanger for my dress?" Eva asked. "I hate to impose on you like this."

"It's okay. There are hangers in my closet," I said. Then I wished I had opened the door myself, because as soon as she looked inside, she was greeted by a pile of sweaty clothes on the floor and two old pairs of sneakers.

She coughed.

"Sorry," I said, scooping up all the clothes and taking them out to the hamper in the hallway.

I left her alone, then, and when she came back downstairs she was wearing a white tee, a short white pleated tennis skirt, and white panties with lace around the legs. She had exchanged her gold earrings for a pair of tiny pearls, and she wore a white terry cloth headband around her shiny black hair. I saw the way Lester's face lit up when she came back in the living room. What I was really conscious of, though, was how skinny she looked. Her elbows and knees were points, not curves, and I decided she looked a lot better in a dress. But Lester was all smiles.

"Have a good game," Dad said. "You two don't seem to mind the heat."

"It will feel great after being in air-conditioning all day," Eva said, and they left the house.

I settled back in the beanbag chair with my book. "So what do you think?" I asked Dad.

"About what?"

"About *her*."

"I don't know her at all, Al, so I don't have an opinion one way or another," he said.

"Yeah, but what's your first impression?"

"First impressions can be misleading."

"Oh, stop being so polite, Dad," I said. "What do you *think* think?"

"That she's an attractive woman and I can see that Lester would be impressed."

"She's not Marilyn," I said. "She's not Crystal."

"Of course she's not. And Sylvia's not your mother, Al. No one can ever take the place of someone else, but that doesn't mean they can't be special in some way."

Whoa! I thought. Who said anything about Mom? Who said anything about Miss Summers? Then I noticed that Dad was holding an opened envelope with a foreign stamp on it, and I knew right away it was from Sylvia Summers. I looked at his face. He didn't look at all upset. He looked pretty happy, in fact.

"Dad?" I asked. "Is there something I should know?"

"About what?"

"You know exactly what. About you and Miss Summers."

"Only that I'm looking forward very much to visiting her. And I think she's looking forward to having me there."

Older people talk so weird, I swear! *Looking forward very much to visiting her.* Translation: *I'm crazy about her.*

"Well, good!" I said. "I hope you have a great time. What will you do while you're there?"

"I suppose we'll travel around and see different places—York, Bath, London, of course; you can see a lot of England in two weeks."

"Miss Summers is in Chester?"

"Yes."

"Does she have an apartment, or is she staying in a room somewhere?"

"It's a small flat. Small, but very British, she says."

"One bedroom or two?"

"Al . . . !" said Dad.

"*What?* I was only asking about her apartment."

"I know what you were asking," he said, and took the letter up to his room. But I could tell that whatever was in it made him happy.

Boy, Sylvia, you'd better not let him down! I thought. *Don't you get my dad all the way over to England and then decide you don't love him.*

It was later, when Dad was in the kitchen making lasagna, that I decided I'd better go upstairs and make sure the bathroom was clean enough for Eva when she came back to take a shower. I took a bath towel and wiped out the tub, pulled a wad of hair out of the drain, wiped the hem of my T-shirt along the edge of the sink, and sprayed a whiff of deodorizer in the air for good measure.

But when I finished, I knew what I had really come upstairs to do. I went to the door of Dad's bedroom and looked in, and there was Miss Summers's letter on his dresser. I felt my pulse pick up and my palms get sweaty.

That is not your business! I told myself. I knew that if I ever got a letter from Patrick, I wouldn't want Dad or Lester reading it. But I felt I had to know. My feet moved forward until they reached the dresser, and I had the letter in my hand.

I compromised. I would not read the letter itself, only the way she signed her name. That, I felt, would tell me all I needed to know without reading any personal details. I moved to the door again and looked down the stairs to make sure Dad was still in the kitchen. Then I took the letter from the opened envelope and unfolded the bottom.

. . . *my arms again,* read the last line. *All my love, Sylvia.*

Yes!

I put the letter back on Dad's dresser in its envelope and went to my own room, where I sat on the edge of my bed, an insane grin on my face. *All my love* meant one hundred percent. It meant there couldn't be any left over for Jim Sorringer. It meant she'd given her heart to Dad. At least, it *better* mean that, I told myself.

•   •   •

I was helping Dad layer the noodles and cheese and sauce, noodles . . . cheese . . . sauce, when Lester and Eva came back from the tennis court. Eva was actually perspiring. Her face glistened, her hair was messed up, and a few wet strands hung limply down over her forehead. There was even a smudge of mascara below her left eye. But she still looked good. I imagined having Eva for a sister-in-law, how she would teach me to look good under any condition. It was hard to imagine.

"Well, she almost beat me," Lester said, pulling a towel from around his neck and wiping his fore-head. "She's a pro."

"Hardly!" said Eva, laughing.

"You can take the first shower," Les told her. "I'll wait. I want to sit out on the back porch and cool off."

Eva went upstairs, and it wasn't until I heard the shower running that I realized I hadn't put out any fresh towels. I hadn't even given her a robe or anything to wear from the bathroom to my bed-room.

I went up to the linen closet and got out a huge beach towel she could wrap up in, then sat down at the top of the stairs to wait and make myself useful. The water cut off at last. I waited . . . and waited . . . and waited some more. Finally the bathroom door opened, and I stood up, holding the towel. When Eva came out, however, she was wearing the bottom half of her white linen dress and had one of our old towels around the top of her. I felt embarrassed. I hoped it wasn't Lester's old smelly towel she'd had to use.

"I'm going to put my makeup on in your room, Alice, so Les can have the shower," she said. "Could you tell him? It's perfectly all right for you to come in your room if you want. I don't mean to take it over."

"I thought you might need another towel," I said, following her to my room, and she quickly accepted. "Lester!" I yelled out the window. "You can have the shower now." Then I sat on the edge of my bed and watched as she spread her cosmetics out on my dresser. She had enough bottles and jars and tubes to make up every actress in Hollywood, I thought. She didn't look quite so much like a porcelain doll without her makeup, but she was still gorgeous.

She frowned at herself in the mirror, then went over to adjust my window shade so she'd have more light. She set to work smearing some kind of gel all over her face. "How old are you now, Alice?" she asked. Even her voice was gorgeous.

"Fourteen," I told her.

"Need any makeup samples? I could get you anything you like."

"Sure," I said, even though I don't wear very much. "Whatever you think I need."

"Certainly not a lot, because you have beautiful coloring," she told me. "But a little moisturizer, a little makeup base and blush . . . powder . . . a bit of eye liner and eyebrow pencil—it works wonders."

"I'd never know how to put it on right, though," I told her.

"Hey, I'd be glad to give you a makeover. Really! We could set one up sometime, and I'd bring all my samples," she said.

"Really?" I thought immediately of Elizabeth and Pamela. "I've got these two great friends. Maybe the three of us could—"

She laughed. "How'd I get roped into doing three? It's okay, though. I'll give you a call sometime when I know I'm coming over."

"That would be great!" I said. Maybe Lester *should* marry this woman.

That night I had a dream that frightened me so that I was almost sick to my stomach when I woke up. I dreamed that Lester was climbing a mountain and his foot slipped. I *saw* it slip. Somehow I was there. I had put out my hand to stop his fall, but I couldn't, and then I was falling with him. When I opened my eyes, I was trying to sit up in bed, and couldn't tell if I'd screamed or not.

What if this was an omen? What if Lester fell off Longs Peak for real?

That afternoon, after my work at the hospital, I stopped at an army surplus store on Georgia Avenue and, the next day, when Lester was packing to leave for the Rockies, I walked in his room and handed him a small packet. "For you," I said.

"Huh? What's this?" he asked.

"Just put it in your bag, Lester, but promise you'll open it before you climb Longs Peak," I told him.

"What is it?"

"Never mind. You'll find out. Just take it."

"Hey, Al. No time for games. I hardly have room for my hiking boots. What *is* it?"

When I still wouldn't answer, Lester opened the sack and stared. "Rope?"

"It's got hooks on each end, Lester. I want you to promise you'll hook onto something when you're climbing the peak."

"Al! I—"

"I *know* you, Lester! You'll try to be real macho and climb without a rope, but . . . the man said it's not real mountain-climbing rope, it's monkey line or something, but it would hold a horse, and all you have to do is hook it onto—"

"Al!"

I stopped.

"We're not using rope. I walk. I don't climb hand over hand. I'm not dangling."

"But on TV, I—"

"I'm not on TV. I'm in a national park with a good friend doing something we've talked about for a couple of years, and if I had a rope around my waist, the way you want, I'd probably trip on it and go stumbling off the edge of the precipice. Okay?"

I swallowed. "I don't want anything to happen to you, Lester," I said in a small voice. "I mean . . . we've lost Mom, and I—"

Lester walked over and gave me a quick hug. "Okay, babe, here's something to remember when you worry that I'm recklessly, stupidly, carelessly walking too near the edge and my foot is going to slip: *I* don't want to die, either. I have as much interest in keeping myself alive as you do. More, in fact. So I expect to be right here in a week, pinning your ears back as usual."

I sniffled and hugged him, too. "Okay," I said, then added, "and kissing Eva?"

"What?"

"You'll be back in a week as usual and go on kissing Eva?"

"Why not?"

"No reason. I just thought . . . maybe she gets makeup on your collars or something."

Lester blinked and shook his head. "You know what, Al? Sometimes you're really weird. Weird and getting weirder," he said.

"I know," I told him. "It's one of my talents. It's what I do best."

6

Hiding Pamela

Pamela and Elizabeth and I kept getting up early to go running. Pamela's already slim, so all our running only made her look better, muscles toned. Frankly, I couldn't see that it made much difference in me—my waist and thighs, maybe. The biggest change was in Elizabeth. We'd been running now for about three weeks, and she had already lost the pudginess under her chin and in her cheeks. I could definitely see an improvement in the size of her stomach.

So it really surprised me once, when Pamela and Elizabeth and Karen and Jill and I were at the mall together, that Elizabeth casually announced she wouldn't be going out with Justin Collier for a while. We'd just started down an escalator and we turned and looked up at Elizabeth, standing behind us.

"What do you mean, for a *while?* Are you going to Siberia or something?" I asked.

"I'm not dating anyone until I lose more weight, and I'm especially not dating Justin, after what he said about me," Elizabeth declared.

Jill frankly stared. "Are you completely nuts? Justin's only the cutest guy in the whole school. Just give the word, Liz, and I'll go after him myself."

"We weren't actually going together or anything," Elizabeth said.

"But he *likes* you! He took you to the dance! Elizabeth, what is your *problem?*" Karen asked.

"I'm fat," Elizabeth said. "He called me chubby. I'm not going out with *any*one until I slim down."

Karen, who's been slim all her life, I guess, said, "Boy, I wish we could trade problems. I'm always drinking malteds to put on weight—malteds with peanut butter in them, even—and as soon as I put on half a pound, I lose it again. Mom's the same way. So's my grandmother."

"What's Justin supposed to do, Elizabeth?" I asked. "Sit home waiting for you to lose weight?"

"That's up to him. He wants me to be thin, I'll be thin. But I won't go out with someone who thinks I'm fat."

"Will you shut up about fat, Elizabeth? You aren't even borderline," said Pamela.

"Not to me," Elizabeth answered.

Karen giggled. "I've got an idea. Let's go over to

my house and I'll call Justin and find out how he really feels about Elizabeth."

We all started laughing, and looked at Elizabeth. She just shrugged. "I don't care," she said.

Karen lives with her mom in an apartment, and her mom was at work. We sat around her living room while she looked up Justin's phone number.

"Hey, doesn't he work?" I asked.

"He should be home by now," said Karen, and dialed his number.

Justin's dad answered. Karen held the phone out away from her so we could all hear.

"Yes, just a minute, I'll get him," he said.

Karen giggled and rolled her eyes at us, and then she was saying, "Hi, Justin. It's Karen. What's happening?"

Justin has a soft voice, so it was difficult to hear what he said, but we all crowded around.

"Yeah, I know what you mean," Karen was saying, straightening out the phone cord. "The heat's brutal. . . . Oh, nothing much. A bunch of us went to the mall this afternoon. . . . Yeah, Elizabeth was there. . . . That's probably why you couldn't reach her, then. . . . Yeah, she told us. I don't know what's the matter with her, Justin. She's got this thing about weight. . . ."

Karen! Elizabeth mouthed.

But Karen barreled on: "I don't know what you

said to her, but she. . . . I *know!* We've all told her, but—"

Suddenly Jill grabbed the phone out of Karen's hand and, raising her voice just a little, speaking a little more breathy, she said, "Hi, Justin, it's me. Elizabeth."

"Jill!" Elizabeth hissed, lunging for the phone, but Jill turned her back. She honestly *did* sound like Elizabeth.

"Oh, Karen's just kidding around," Jill said. There was a long pause, and we all wished we could hear what Justin was saying. "Okay, then," Jill said finally. "What *do* you like about me?"

Elizabeth covered her face with her hands.

"My eyes, yes . . ." Jill repeated, grinning and nodding toward the rest of us. "My hair . . . my *what?*" She opened her mouth in surprise, and motioned toward her butt. We were sure Jill was making it up, and Pamela grabbed the phone from her hands.

"Justin, that was Jill, not Elizabeth, and this is Pamela . . . yeah, I know you're confused. So are we. We are the most confused and confusing girls in Silver Spring. . . . No, it wasn't Elizabeth's idea to call. You want to talk to her?"

Elizabeth violently shook her head and backed away. Pamela giggled.

"He says to say hello to everybody in the room,

but he and his parents are heading out for dinner," Pamela told us. "Bye, Justin."

"Bye, Justin!" Jill and Karen and I screeched.

"You guys, that was so stupid!" Elizabeth said after we'd hung up.

"That's what *he* said," Pamela reported, laughing.

"Now that everybody in this room has flirted with Justin Collier, can we go home?" I asked, and Pamela, Elizabeth, and I said good-bye. If this wasn't the best summer we'd ever had, it was certainly the silliest, I decided.

It wasn't just exercising that was slimming Elizabeth down, though. Pamela and I discovered she wasn't eating. Not much, anyway. When we'd order a pizza, for example, she'd take only one slice and pull the cheese off the top before she ate it. She carried this little calorie book around with her, and she wouldn't take a bite of anything until she'd checked it out.

"I can eat all the strawberries and melons I want," she said. "And I can have any vegetables, except potatoes, corn, and peas."

"Oh, boy, that'll fill you up," I said. "You know, Elizabeth, half a bagel now and then wouldn't hurt you."

"And skim milk," said Elizabeth. "I can have that, too."

"What about eating everything you normally would and just taking smaller portions?" asked Pamela.

"Too risky," said Elizabeth. "Once I had a taste of chocolate, for instance, I wouldn't be able to stop."

"What are you, a perpetual motion machine?" I asked her. "You're not on automatic, Elizabeth. You can tell yourself to stop."

"I know what I'm doing," said Elizabeth.

The fact was, I don't think any of us knew what we were doing. The summer between eighth and ninth grades was turning out to be the SMC— Summer of Mass Confusion. I was moody with Dad and Lester because they got to go somewhere and I didn't; Elizabeth was having fights with her mom over food, she told us; and Pamela was fighting with her dad.

Pamela said that ever since her mom left, it was as though her dad were trying to lose her too. When she did something he didn't like, he'd say, "You're going to turn out just like your mother," and that really ticked her off.

"If you don't want me around, just say so," she'd tell him.

But he did want her around, and told her so. It was just that they both blew up over every little thing.

On the Fourth of July, Patrick's folks were entertaining a diplomat's family and wanted him to be there. All my other friends were off with their families doing something different. Dad and I did something different, all right. We watched the fireworks on TV. We really know how to party.

The following night, though, about ten o'clock, I was folding the laundry when I got a call from Pamela: "Alice, don't ask any questions, just meet me at the corner by the mailbox in fifteen minutes, okay? And don't tell anyone."

"What's going on?" I asked.

"I'll see you at the mailbox," was all she said, and hung up.

Now what? I wondered.

Dad was watching an old Spencer Tracy movie on PBS, and at ten-fifteen, I called, "I'm going down to the mailbox, Dad. Be back in a couple minutes."

"Okay," he answered.

I got there before Pamela, but then I saw her under the street light a block away, walking toward me with a small overnight bag in her hand. I went up the sidewalk to meet her. "What's happening?" I asked.

"Alice, you've got to do me a huge favor," she said. "I want to stay at your place tonight and I don't want anyone to know. Not even your dad or Lester."

"Lester's in the Rockies."

"Well, I don't want my father to find out where I am. We had this really big fight after dinner, and I walked out."

"Where did you go? Where have you been all this time?"

"Sitting in the Greyhound terminal, but I don't want to stay there overnight."

"You *know* he'll call here!" I told her.

"That's why I don't want your dad to know. You've got to smuggle me inside your house and I'll leave early tomorrow morning. No one has to know I'm there."

"Pamela!" I said. "I can't!"

"If you don't, I'll go back to the bus station and spend the night there."

I looked at Pamela in her short shorts and halter top, and knew that the last place she should be spending the night was a bus station.

I sighed. "All right. Wait outside till I give the signal and I'll sneak you in the back door. If Dad's still watching TV in the living room, you can come up to my room without his seeing you."

We walked back to my house; I took a deep breath and went in. "Hey, Dad, want me to make you some popcorn?" I asked, hoping the noise of the air popper would drown out the creak of the hallway stairs.

"Oh, I don't think so. It's too hot for popcorn. If you feel like making milk shakes, though, I'll take one of those," he said.

"Sure." The blender was even better.

I went out in the kitchen and poured milk and chocolate syrup in the blender, then added ice cream and turned it to high speed. I went to the back door and signaled Pamela.

Tiptoeing down the hall, I peeked in to see if Dad was still in front of the TV, then motioned Pamela out of the kitchen and she sneaked upstairs. I went back in the kitchen and turned off the blender.

"One milk shake coming up!" I said, taking it in to Dad.

"Thanks, honey. Aren't you having one?"

"Yeah. I'll make another for myself."

"If you've never watched a Spencer Tracy movie, you'd like this one—*Bad Day at Black Rock*," he said. "Sure you don't want to watch? I could fill you in. . . ."

"No, I've got a good book to read," I told him.

"Enjoy!" he said, and settled back down.

I made another large milk shake, divided it between two glasses, and went upstairs. As soon as I got in my room, I closed the door behind me.

"What happened?" I asked again, handing Pamela

one of the glasses. "And we've got to whisper."

She seemed more angry than anything else. "I'm going to teach Dad a lesson he'll never forget," she said. "He won't let me do anything! Some of the bikers from school rode by, and I was just sitting out on the porch talking to them. We weren't doing *any*thing, and he came out and practically dragged me inside. He *humiliated* me!"

I knew all about being humiliated on the front porch. But I also know that when a girl says she "wasn't doing anything," what she sometimes means is "yet."

Pamela continued: "Dad and I were absolutely screaming at each other, and he called me a slut. He said I'd turn out just like Mom. I slapped him, and he slapped me back." She swallowed. "We've . . . neither of us . . . ever done that before. Afterward he went out back to smoke, and I just threw some things in a bag and went to the bus station. Let him worry all night long, I don't care. It'll serve him right."

She took a long drink of the milk shake, and I wondered if she could even taste it. She was sitting cross-legged on my bed, and I sat at the other end with my shake, facing her.

"It's okay to stay here, but you can't run over without telling him every time you have an argument," I said.

"I know, but this was the worst fight we've ever had."

I sat there studying Pamela, listening to the movie sounds drifting up from downstairs, feeling pretty lucky, I guess, that Dad and I get along as well as we do.

"How are you going to use the bathroom?" I asked. Trust me to come up with practical questions, but, like Patrick says, I'm practical. "If Dad knew you were here, Pamela, he'd freak out."

"I don't know. I'll just use the john once before I go to bed and again in the morning, and then I'll leave," she said. "I can brush my teeth in here."

I leaned back against the headboard. "What's happening to us, Pamela? You and Elizabeth and me? This was supposed to be a great summer."

There were tears in her eyes. "I know," she said, and her voice was as high as a kitten's mew. "I don't want to go live with Mom, but all Dad and I seem to do anymore is fight." She began to cry.

"You're both sad and miserable," I told her.

"And angry. That's what I am most," she wept. "Sometimes I think I really hate Mom for what she's done to Dad and me. All she cares about is herself."

I just listened. There wasn't anything, really, that I could say. I wished I'd asked Lester to look up Mrs. Jones while he was in Colorado and tell her what she was doing to Pamela.

I decided I'd better check on Dad, so I took our glasses down to the kitchen, making sure I rinsed them out and put them away. Then I went in the living room to collect Dad's glass. He was just turning off the TV.

"Want another one?" I asked.

"Oh, no. I've had enough," he said. "Say, how's it going at the hospital, Al? Anything interesting?"

"Pretty much the same. I was in the hall when an emergency came in the other day. Just like *ER*—people yelling and banging doors open and attendants and tubes and everything."

"Well, it's a broadening experience. Everything new that you can experience will only make you wiser."

"*Everything?*" I teased. "I can think of plenty of experiences you don't want me to have."

He gave me a look, and we were about to joke some more when the phone rang. I went out in the hall and took it before Dad could answer.

"Alice?" came Elizabeth's voice. "Mr. Jones just called and wanted to know if Pamela was over here. He says she went out earlier and hasn't come back!"

"Really?" I said. "When was that?"

"Around seven, he thinks."

"Did he . . . was she mad or something?"

"He said some boys came by and Pamela was out on the porch with them, and then he and Pamela quarreled."

"Oh, she's probably walking it off," I said. "I bet she'll show up."

"Well, *you're* awfully calm about it," Elizabeth said. "From his description, I'll bet those guys were bikers from school. I'll bet she rode off with them and they're having sex somewhere, just to spite her father."

Elizabeth's imagination was off and running. I was tempted to tell her where Pamela was but, knowing Elizabeth, I was sure she'd feel guilty if she didn't tell Mr. Jones. If she tried to keep it secret, she'd end up at confession on Saturday apologizing for me, too, and I didn't want to put her through that.

"What do you think we should do?" asked Elizabeth.

"I don't know," I told her.

"Mr. Jones said he was going to get in his car and go looking for her. Maybe we ought to go with him."

"I don't think so," I told Elizabeth. "I think we ought to stay right where we are, so that if she calls either one of us, we'll be home."

"Okay. But if you hear anything, let me know," Elizabeth said. "I'm really worried about her." And she hung up. Now there were two people worried about Pamela.

Dad stood in the living room doorway. "What was that all about?"

"Elizabeth says that Pamela had a fight with her dad and stormed out, and he's looking for her. My guess is that she's walking around the block."

"Sort of late for her to be out, though, isn't it?" Dad said. "They've sure had their share of trouble lately."

"I guess so," I said.

"Al," he said, "if you're ever mad at me, don't run off. Stay and argue, okay? Easier on my digestion."

"Okay, if *you* promise not to run off with a NordicTrack instructor," I said.

"No danger of that," said Dad.

I grinned. "How do I know you won't go to England to see Miss Summers and decide to stay?"

"I'd come back just to see what you and Les were up to," Dad told me.

When I went back upstairs, I closed my door after me and motioned for Pamela to be quiet. I threw my spread on the floor on the other side of the bed and made her sit down there in case Dad came up.

"Who was on the phone?" she whispered.

"Elizabeth," I whispered back, and told her what she'd said about Pamela's dad.

"Good! He's worried! I hope he's up all night," Pamela said.

"You really should go home, Pamela. This won't solve anything," I told her.

"Well, we weren't solving anything before, so what have I got to lose?" she asked.

"His trust?"

But Pamela only stretched out with her arms behind her head and stared up at the ceiling.

7

Blowup

We had to have a plan.

"Dad comes in the room, you've got to roll under the bed," I told her. "I mean it, Pamela. If he knew you were here—"

"It's only for this one night," she promised.

I kept my door half open so I could hear Dad if he came upstairs. Then I lay on my side on the bed, looking down at Pamela.

"Do you suppose life is always going to be like this?" she asked after a while.

"I don't know. Dad says that life is what happens to you when you're planning something else," I said. "Like with Mom. They had all kinds of plans, and then, she died."

"Great! Just great!" said Pamela.

The phone rang again, and Dad answered from downstairs.

"Al," he called. "It's Pamela's father. He wants to speak with you."

"Don't tell him *anything!*" Pamela whispered.

I went out in the hall and picked up the upstairs phone. "Hello?"

"Alice, this is Mr. Jones. I wondered if Pamela might be over there."

"Over *here?*" I asked. And when he didn't answer, I said, "Was she coming here? What time did she leave?" I was trying hard not to out-and-out lie.

"Well, she left the house some time ago, but she didn't say where she was going. I thought you might have seen her." I could tell he was worried.

"Have you checked with Elizabeth?" I said. "Maybe she went there."

"Elizabeth hasn't seen her, either."

"Gee, I'm sorry, Mr. Jones. Have you tried Jill or Karen?"

"I don't have their numbers. If you could give them to me . . ."

I felt like pig slop, the way I was leading him on, reciting those phone numbers knowing very well that it wouldn't help.

"Thanks, Alice. If she turns up there, will you tell her I'm worried about her and ask her to call home?"

"I sure will," I promised.

I went back in the bedroom. "Your dad's really worried, Pamela. He said if you come here, I should ask you to call home," I whispered.

"In a pig's eye!" she said.

I heard Dad coming upstairs, so I shook Pamela's knee. She rolled over on her stomach and wiggled under my bed, pulling the spread with her.

Dad tapped on the door and stuck his head inside. "Any news about Pamela?" he asked.

"Only that she hasn't come back yet. I gave him Karen's and Jill's numbers."

"He must be worried sick," said Dad.

"Elizabeth and I figure the best thing we can do is stay put in case she comes here. I can't think of anyplace else she'd go."

"Well, I'm going to bed," said Dad. "I'm sure *her* dad won't get much sleep tonight. See you in the morning."

He went back to his room and shut the door. Pamela and I lay there whispering for a while. We could hear Dad moving around, opening a drawer, scooting a chair.

"I have to pee," Pamela said.

"Well, you can't do it now," I told her. "Dad always puts his pajamas on first, then goes in the bathroom to wash up and brush his teeth."

"I have to go really bad, Alice! You might have to get me a bedpan or something."

"A *bedpan?*"

"A chamber pot, then."

"What?"

"A bucket. Whatever."

I was beginning to think this might be the best solution, when I heard the doorbell ring.

"Al, was that the doorbell?" called Dad.

"I think so."

"Wait. I'll get it," he said. "I don't want you opening the door yourself at this time of night, though it could be Pamela, of course. . . ."

The doorbell rang again, followed by several light knocks. Dad came by my door in his bathrobe and turned on the hall light, then went down.

I crawled across the bedroom floor on my hands and knees so I could see into the hall below where Dad had opened the door. I could see his feet, and the feet and pants of another man. Then I heard a stranger's voice saying, "Sorry to bother you, Mr. McKinley, but we've got a missing person's report from Mr. Jones, who says your two daughters are friends. We don't usually investigate until a kid's been missing a lot longer than this, but he's pretty worried, and we thought we'd ask around. Wonder if I could come in for a minute and talk to Alice."

"Pamela!" I croaked, tumbling back into the bedroom. "It's the police!"

"Good!" she said.

"Are you nuts? He wants to talk to me!" I whispered. "What if he wants to search the house?"

"He has to have a search warrant," said Pamela.

"Al?" came Dad's voice. "Are you dressed? Could you come down for a minute?"

"What am I going to *say?*" I squeaked to Pamela.

"You haven't seen me! You don't know a thing!" she insisted.

"Coming!" I called.

I went downstairs in my cutoffs and tank top. The officer was standing in our living room. He came over and put out his hand. "Hello, Alice," he said. "Mr. Jones tells me you're a friend of his daughter's. I think he told you that she left the house after dinner and hasn't come back, and there's one worried dad over there. He seems to think she might have gone off with some boys who came by earlier, but he doesn't know any of their names. We wondered if you could give me names and addresses—just to make sure Pamela's okay."

I concentrated on looking concerned without looking nervous.

"The bikers? Uh . . . "

"Excuse me?"

"They were probably the bikers. That's what we call them at school, the guys who ride mountain bikes to school and ride around the parking lot during lunch period. But I don't know any of their names."

"Would any of your friends know these boys?"

"Uh . . . some of the guys might, I'm not sure."

This was horrible! I could imagine the policeman going around to all my friends and waking their parents and . . .

"When was the last time you spoke with Pamela yourself?" the officer asked.

I'd hoped I wouldn't have to come right out and lie. So far I'd just sort of skirted the truth, but now I'd been asked a direct question.

"Uh . . . today?" I said. "I'm not sure. I knew she and her dad had quarreled."

"She called you then?"

"Yes, she told me they'd quarreled."

"And about what time would that be?"

Suddenly I saw Dad stiffen.

"Excuse me," he said, and headed rapidly for the stairs.

What? What had he heard? I wondered. And then I realized that the toilet had flushed.

The next thing I knew, there was a small shriek from upstairs, a murmur of voices, and then I could see Dad's feet descending the stairs along with Pamela's.

"Officer," said Dad, "I think this is the young lady you're looking for." He had a death grip on

Pamela's arm, but the look he gave me was one I would never forget. I couldn't tell if it was more anger or disappointment.

Pamela stared helplessly at the policeman, then at me.

"You flushed!" I told her.

"I know! I realized too late!" she wailed.

The officer put his notebook away. "You're Pamela?"

She nodded.

"Your dad is awfully worried about you," he said. For the first time that evening, Pamela didn't say *good.* "Let me say something," the policeman went on. "I know that parents and kids quarrel from time to time; I sure had enough quarrels with my own dad. But I also know what can happen to girls out on the street when they run away, even for one night. I'm glad you stayed with a friend, but you'd have to be a parent yourself, I guess, to understand how concerned your father is about you."

Pamela didn't say anything.

"I don't know what you quarreled about, but I'm sure you and your dad can work it out." And when Pamela went on staring at her feet, he added, "I'd like to drive you home."

Pamela shrugged. "I'll get my stuff in the morning, Alice," she murmured.

"Okay," I told her, my chest cold.

"Thanks, folks," the policeman said, and shut the door behind them.

I was almost afraid to look at Dad, but suddenly I found myself being jerked around, facing him, and I'd never seen his face that angry. "You *lied* to me!" he shouted.

"I . . . I . . . no, I didn't."

"You lied to me in everything you did tonight, making me believe you didn't know where she was."

I thought he was going to slap me, that we would end up just like Pamela and her dad, but he didn't. I was trying to back away from him, but he had hold of both my arms and shook me.

"This is the second time you've shown me you can't be trusted, and I can't tell you how disappointed I am." He gave my arms a final thrust as though he were too disgusted to even touch me, and I felt as though my whole body had been plunged in ice water. I couldn't bear that he was so angry with me, but I knew he was right. I knew without asking that he was talking about the day he had forbidden me to go to school with green mousse on my head, and my hair in spikes, and I'd done it, anyway.

"Dad, she was really, really upset. Pamela called me from the bus station and said that—"

"I don't *care* what she said!" Dad yelled. "I care

that for five hours or so Mr. Jones has been worried sick about his daughter. You knew it, and yet you hid her right up there under my nose. What do you take me for, Alice, a fool?"

I was crying, but it didn't bother Dad.

"He . . . he slapped her," I whimpered, without telling Dad, of course, that she'd slapped him first.

"At this point I'd almost believe she deserved it," Dad went on. "Here I am, getting ready to leave you and Lester by yourselves for two weeks in August, and if this is what happens when I'm here, what on earth can I expect when I'm gone? How can I believe a thing you tell me when I get back?"

"Dad . . .!" I was really crying then. "I'm sorry! I'm so sorry! I knew she shouldn't be here! I told her that! But she was so mad at him, and . . . and wanted to teach him a lesson . . . and . . . and . . . she said she'd only do it this one time, and—"

"Well, it taught *me* a lesson, all right. I can't trust my own daughter. This disgusts me, Alice! Mr. Jones and the policeman both must think I'm an idiot, all this going on in my own house!"

He wasn't listening to me, so there was no point in talking anymore. I just stood there in the hall crying.

"Go to bed," he said finally. "I'm going to call your aunt Sally tomorrow and ask her to come stay here while I'm in England."

Oh, no! Not Aunt Sally, who still lives in the Dark Ages! I sobbed in earnest as I went upstairs. There was no good night kiss from Dad. No hug. The two unchaperoned weeks I was planning to have with Patrick were down the tube. Aunt Sally was the World's Original Chaperone, with more rules than the U.S. Navy. Worse than that, when Lester found out that Aunt Sally would be here to chaperone him, too, *he'd* hate me.

I was in and out of sleep all night. I kept hoping Dad might come in and sit on the edge of my bed and we'd quietly talk it out. But he didn't. I didn't have the nerve to go in and talk to him because I knew how angry he must be. Having Aunt Sally come to our house, however, was the ultimate punishment. She not only wouldn't let me be alone with Patrick, she probably wouldn't even allow him on the porch. To hear Aunt Sally talk, all you had to do was put a boy and a girl in a room alone together and there was an instant, magnetic mating pull. They simply couldn't help themselves. There would be only one possible thing they could think of doing, and that was sexual intercourse.

Pamela didn't come over to go running the next morning, of course. I heard the phone ring; I heard Dad answer out in the hallway, and I heard him say, "She's still sleeping, Elizabeth. You'll have to call later."

I purposely stayed in bed until I felt sure he had left for work. Then I went downstairs in my pajamas thinking maybe he'd left a loving note for me on the table or something. Instead, I found Dad still there, reading the *Post*.

"Sit down," he said.

I sat.

"You are going to be grounded for a week," he said. "You can leave the house only the three times you volunteer at the hospital. You are to go directly there and home again. No stops on the way."

I swallowed. "What . . . about my job at the Melody Inn?" I was thinking of the three hours I put in on Saturday mornings at Dad's music store. "Should I . . . should I come in this morning?"

"All right, four times. You can go to work at the store. But other than those, you are not to leave the property. You cannot go to the Stedmeisters' pool, you can't go out for ice cream, and you are not to have friends here."

I couldn't believe the severity of my punishment. "Not even Elizabeth?"

"Not even her."

I burst into tears. "You are so unfair! You don't even listen to my explanations! You don't even *care* what Pamela might be going through. You're just mad because she was here and you didn't know it. You only care how that made *you* look!"

"You're darn right I care! Put yourself in my place, Alice! How would you feel if I smuggled Sylvia in the house and pretended she wasn't here? Is this a family or not? Can we trust each other or not? Apparently we can't."

He got up and rinsed out his coffee cup. "I'm going to work," he said, and left the house.

I curled up in my beanbag chair in the living room and bawled. I was angry at Dad, even angrier at myself, and positively furious at Pamela for getting me into this.

Elizabeth called. "What's happening?" she said. "Dad said he saw a patrol car parked in front of your house last night around eleven-thirty."

"It's awful!" I wept, and told her everything—the phone call from Pamela, the way I got her upstairs, how Mr. Jones had called here, the visit from the police, how angry Dad was with me, and that I was grounded for a week.

I'd thought that Elizabeth, of all people, would be sympathetic, but after a long pause, all she said was, "You *lied?* To your own *father?*"

"But . . . but Pamela was . . ."

"You broke two of the commandments right there."

"What?"

"Lying, and dishonoring your father."

"Elizabeth, I'm in no mood to be preached at!" I told her. "Pamela was mad at me when she left, I'm mad at myself, Dad is furious with me, Lester will disown me, and now you've got God mad at me, too."

"I know how you feel, Alice, but I'm only quoting the Bible," Elizabeth said.

I closed my eyes and slowly let my body slide down the wall there in the hallway until I was sitting flat on the floor. "Bring on the floods! Bring on the locusts!" I wailed, remembering what few Bible stories I knew. "Let the plagues begin!"

8

A Heated Discussion

It was the first time I can remember that Dad and I stayed mad at each other for more than a day. Saturday was horrible because we avoided each other at the Melody Inn. Both Janice Sherman and Marilyn noticed, but didn't say anything. Patrick was out of town with his folks for the weekend, so I couldn't even talk with him. When Lester came home on Sunday, Dad and I still weren't speaking much.

"Well," I said, when Les came in the house with a week's growth of beard on his face, sunburned but happy. "You didn't fall off a peak."

"Oh, man, it was great!" Lester told me. "I'm feeling muscles I didn't even know I had. I need about twenty years to catch up on sleep, but I'd do it again in a heartbeat."

At dinner, he told us how they'd had to get up at three in the morning to reach the base of the trail so they could get to the summit and start back before two in the afternoon, when storms were most likely to move in. How they'd taken a couple tins of smoked oysters and caviar to eat at the top in celebration. How they'd fallen into bed at the end of each day's climb without even bothering to bathe, they were so tired.

"Sounds like a very physical vacation," Dad said, smiling at Lester. "Discovering new things about yourself. A stretch, they say."

Knives clunked against plates, glasses clinked on the table, and we were all, I guess, a little too conscious of the hum of the refrigerator. At some point I saw Lester pause and steal a quick look at Dad, who was slowly, methodically, cutting up a piece of flank steak. Then Lester turned his head and stared quizzically at me. I went on stabbing my lima beans, putting them in my mouth one by one.

"Did somebody die?" Lester asked finally, looking from me to Dad and back again, like he was watching a tennis match.

"Not that I'm aware of," said Dad, and continued eating.

Lester took another couple of bites. "Did I miss something?" he asked. "Someone moving out, maybe?"

"No, it just hasn't been a very cheerful place the last few days, Les," said Dad. He stood up and took his dishes to the sink. "Al can fill you in. I want to do some yard work before it gets dark." He went out the back door, and we could hear him fumbling about the toolshed.

Lester looked over at me. "Now what?" he asked. "Why do I get the feeling it has something to do with you?"

"It's so unfair, Lester!" I told him. And, for the third time, I spilled out the story.

Lester went right on shoveling food in his mouth as I talked—how Pamela had been hiding here, how Pamela had flushed—until I got to the part about how Dad was going to ask Aunt Sally to come and chaperone us while he was in England. Then Lester half rose from his chair.

"What?" he yelled.

"That's what he said, Lester. I couldn't reason with him! He said I couldn't be trusted, so—"

"So *I* have to suffer? *I* have to put up with Sal snooping through my things and asking what time I'll be home, and giving me subtle hints about sexually transmitted diseases, and leaving clippings about alcohol-related deaths on my dresser? How could you be so stupid to think you could pull something like that on Dad?"

I couldn't take any more. Pamela hadn't called me, Dad was mad at me, Elizabeth was praying for me, and now Lester was against me, too. I leaped up from the table and screeched, "Everyone in the whole world hates me, and I might as well be dead!" Then I dramatically ran upstairs to my room and banged the door so hard that the house shook.

If there was ever a worse summer in my entire life, I don't know when it was. Except maybe the summer Mom was so sick, which I can hardly remember. She died shortly after I started kindergarten, they tell me. Somehow, having both Lester and Dad mad at me at the same time was more than I could bear.

I lay on my bed a long time trying to sort things through. All kinds of thoughts were going through my head. I think I was maddest of all at myself for sabotaging my chance to be alone with Patrick while Dad was away.

Ever since that drum lesson in Patrick's basement when he'd kissed me, and again on our porch, trying a different kind of kiss—a different position, anyway—I'd remembered that *zing* going through my body—that heavy, warm, excited feeling, and it felt good. I wanted to feel it again, and part of the thrill is not knowing what Patrick will do next. I wanted it, and encouraged it, but knew I would never agree to having intercourse. You just sort of want to see how far a guy might go and how far you'll let him before you stop. Which is probably what worries Dad. It's not fair in the least, of course, expecting a boy to make all the moves and the girl to just react to them. How does he know what you want or when to stop? I wouldn't want to be a guy and have all that responsibility for anything in the world.

I finally got up because the phone was ringing and Lester called up the stairs that it was for me. I answered out in the hallway. It was Pamela.

"Alice," she said, "Thanks for letting me come over the other night. I hope I didn't get you in trouble."

"You don't know the half of it," I said bitterly.

"Well, Dad and I had a talk, and I promised I wouldn't run away anymore if he wouldn't keep telling me I was going to turn out just like Mom, so maybe things will be different, I don't know."

"Yeah? Well, now *my* dad's mad at *me!*" I told her. "He was furious at me for not telling him you were up in my room. I *told* you he'd be mad, Pamela, and now I'm grounded for a week."

"Did you tell him it was all my idea?" she asked.

"So what's he supposed to do? Ground *you* for a week? He'd just ask if we were Siamese twins, with one brain doing the thinking for both of us."

"Gosh, I'm sorry, Alice."

"Well, so am I. I can't see any of my friends or go anywhere except the hospital and the Melody Inn."

"We can call, can't we?"

"I guess. He wasn't *that* radical."

After we hung up, I decided I might as well go downstairs. I hadn't had any dessert yet, and I was still hungry. So I found a box of vanilla wafers, poured myself a glass of milk, and took them into the living room. Then I sat down in my beanbag chair, the box of cookies between my knees, and took out a cookie at a time, dipping it in the milk, then stuffing the whole thing in my mouth. *Thrust, crinkle-crinkle, dip, chew; thrust, crinkle-crinkle, dip, chew . . .*

Lester was catching up with a stack of newspapers on the couch. "What are you, an assembly line?" he asked finally.

I didn't answer. I pretended I could turn him into a centipede just by deep concentration.

"Quit glaring at me, Al. I can feel your eyeballs boring through the back of the newspaper," he said.

"Well, you're being just as unreasonable as Dad," I told him. "What if Eva called you some night and said she'd had this big fight with her father and wanted you to smuggle her into *your* room for the night? What would *you* do?"

"She lives in an apartment," came Lester's voice from behind the newspaper.

"But what if she didn't? What if she lived at

home and all her girlfriends were out of town and you were her last great hope?"

Lester slowly lowered his paper and peered at me over the top. "*You* are Pamela's last great hope? Doesn't she have at least a dozen friends?"

"You're dodging the question, Lester. It would be the same moral dilemma regardless of who took her in."

"Do you really think I could have a woman up in my room with Dad here and he wouldn't know about it?" Lester asked.

"Answer the question, Lester."

We heard the back screen slam, and Dad washing his hands in the kitchen.

"Well, even if I did, I'd choose a woman with enough sense not to flush the toilet when everyone else was downstairs," he said.

"You see? See? You would have done the same. It's easy to tell someone else what to do, but . . ." I realized suddenly that Dad was there in the doorway.

"Maybe I should be in on this discussion," he said.

"Maybe you should!" I said, heating up. "Because all you've done is yell at me and tell me *your* feelings, but you haven't listened to mine."

He came on in the living room and sat down at the other end of the couch. "All right. Now that tempers have calmed down a little, maybe this is a good time to talk."

"Speak for yourself," said Lester. "I haven't calmed down. Because of Al, here, and her gnat-brained friend, *I* have to put up with Aunt Sal for two weeks while you're in England?"

Dad sighed. "She isn't coming. She and Ned have already rented a cottage in Michigan the last two weeks of August, and of course I wouldn't expect her to change her plans."

"The earth is fair and the Lord is bountiful!" said Lester, and I felt this huge wave of relief. Relief and excitement.

"I'm ready to hear your side of the story, Al," Dad said.

"Okay. I realize that hiding Pamela in my room was wrong, but when she called me that night, all she said was for me to meet her at the mailbox on the corner. It wasn't till then that she said she wanted to spend the night at our house, that I had to keep it secret, and if I didn't let her she'd go back to the Greyhound bus depot and spend the night there. And I *knew* you wouldn't want her to do that. I *told* her it wouldn't solve anything and that she should go back home, but she wouldn't listen. What should I have *done,* Dad? If I'd said no and she went to sleep on a bench at the depot, and a sex fiend dragged her outside in the alley and raped her and slit her throat, and her father had a heart attack when he heard the news, and her mother committed suicide because she felt it was all her fault for running off with her Nordic-Track instructor, and then I told you it never would have happened if I'd let Pamela stay here where I knew she'd be safe, how would you feel then? Huh? Huh?"

"Would you repeat that again, Al? I think I might have missed something," said Lester.

Dad thought for a minute. "I think, in a situation like that, you should have talked her into coming here without making any promises, and then let me know she was here."

"And betray my friend? You'd go right to the phone and call Mr. Jones, and he'd come and get her, and then she'd run away again and *really* go to the bus depot. Probably buy a ticket and take a bus to somewhere. And you saw what she was wearing, Dad. Those short shorts and halter top! I was just being loyal to a friend, and for that *I* get punished!"

"I didn't say I'd send her home if you'd told me. But I *would* let her father know that she was all right. I'd say she was upset and suggest she be allowed to stay here for a while until things cooled down."

"Oh," I said. I hadn't thought of that. But, of

course, Pamela's whole point in running away was to scare her father silly. If anyone should have been locked up for a week, it was Pamela.

We were all quiet a moment. Then Dad said, "I want you both to know that my going to England to visit Sylvia means a great deal to me. But if I have to worry about what's happening here at home, I won't have a very good time, and neither will she."

"You can trust me, Dad! I won't do anything like that again while you're away, I promise!" I told him.

"I want it strictly understood," he went on, "that no one, *no* one—male or female—is to spend the night here, or *part* of a night here, while I'm gone."

"I promise," I said.

Dad looked at Lester.

"Okay by me," he said, somewhat reluctantly, I imagined. But I knew that wouldn't bother him much. After all, if Eva had her own apartment, Les could spend the night there.

"And I also want it understood," said Dad, "that both of you are to spend every night here, and not just part of a night, either."

I saw Lester swallow. "Define 'night,'" he said.

Dad just gave him a look. "I want you each to look out for the other, but you are basically each responsible for yourself. If there's disagreement, though, Les has the final say. Understood, Alice?"

"Yes," I said. Then I gave *Lester* a look.

"Listen, Dad," Lester told him, "We both want you to have a good time, and you don't have to worry about us. We know not to leave anything cooking on the stove, we'll remember to lock the doors at night, we'll—"

"I'm not concerned about the stove or the doors," Dad said pointedly.

"And I'm not going to do anything with Eva that I wouldn't do if you were right here in town," Lester added.

"I wonder why that isn't particularly comforting," Dad said, but smiled just a little.

Both Dad and I felt better when the discussion was over. He understood the pressure I'd been under to keep Pamela's visit secret; I realized that she still could have stayed here if I'd told Dad about it; and Lester knew he had to stay here at night, and that Eva wasn't part of the game plan while Dad was gone. It was Les who didn't feel any better after the discussion than he had before.

Up in my room later, I was thinking again about Patrick and the two weeks Dad would be gone. I couldn't invite him in, of course, but there was no rule about sitting out on the swing in the dark, just the two of us alone, without Dad watching from the window.

When I heard Lester come up to his room later, I went out and stood in the doorway, watching him unpack all the dirty clothes from his hiking trip. "Eeuuuw! It smells like a week's supply of dirty socks!" I said.

"Ummm. Good. Man smell! Testosterone!" he teased.

"I doubt Eva would care much for it," I told him.

"She doesn't have to like it. She wasn't invited along. You don't take a woman like Eva hiking in the mountains."

I thought about that a minute. "You might have taken Marilyn," I said.

"Marilyn's history," said Lester. "Besides, this was a guy thing."

"Les, how far can you go with a boy before it's considered sex?" I asked.

He threw another pair of socks on the pile and looked at me. "Who are you? Monica Lewinsky?"

"Really. I want to know."

"Hey, babe, sex covers a wide territory. Holding hands can be sexual. Hugging and kissing can be sexual. Hair stroking, arm caressing, back rubbing, foot touching, thigh grazing, knee patting, ear blowing, tongue kissing, finger locking, and eye gazing can all be sexual."

"Huh?" I said.

"Anything that produces a zing, a ping, or a rush is sexual, okay? What *you* want to know, I think, is where do the okays end and the no-nos begin. Right?"

"Well . . ."

"And that's something you have to decide for yourself. Aunt Sal's definition of sex, she told me once, is anything you wouldn't do in front of your parents."

"Which is most of the above," I said, discouraged. "Elizabeth says a nun told her to keep both feet on the floor at all times, but Pamela says only if you keep your knees together."

"Which, of course, leaves the whole upper torso fair game," said Lester. "And it also doesn't deal with the question of what it does to a woman's sexuality if she always goes just so far and then stops. This is what makes human life so interesting, see? If we were animals, we could just roll around and do whatever felt good with whoever came along. But now that we've evolved, now that we've got consciences, and have societies and family structures and stuff, we have to play by the rules. So for the two weeks I'm in charge, please, just don't do anything with Patrick that, if I were to walk out on the porch and turn on the light, would embarrass me. Okay?"

Since Lester doesn't embarrass easily, I figured that gave us plenty of room.

"All right," I said. "Same with you and Eva?"

Lester growled at me. "Get outta here," he said, and threw another pile of clothes on the floor.

9

Grounded

Dad and I were speaking again, but I was still grounded. As he said, Pamela wasn't his responsibility, but I was, and sometimes loyalty to a friend can get in the way of common sense.

The news of my grounding spread fast. I began to realize that almost nothing makes you more popular than to be grounded. Everybody started calling, and I could tell by Dad's reaction that he wished he'd nixed phone calls, too.

"You can't have anyone over?" Jill asked when she called. "Not even Patrick?"

"Especially Patrick," I said, and felt really sorry for myself about that.

"What you need is e-mail," said Karen. "I can't believe you don't have a computer, Alice."

"Lester has one," I told her, not wanting anyone to think we're behind the times, even though we usually get something about a decade after every-one else has it.

"Then you should have your own private e-mail! We could send you all kinds of messages. Ask your brother to set one up for you."

I would, but this didn't exactly seem the right time for it. I was supposed to suffer.

Gwen, though, didn't think it was such a bad punishment. When we rode the bus together Monday, she said if she ever lied to her dad, she'd probably be grounded for a month. "The one thing he won't sit still for," she said. "That and sass talk."

"How many in your family?" I asked.

"Five. Two brothers. Dad's even stricter with them."

"What about your mom?"

"She and Dad must have gone to the same school. They agree all the way down the line," said Gwen.

The week before, I had been on flower and mail delivery at the hospital, and Gwen had been as-signed to physical therapy. Now we were switched, and I helped out in the physical therapy room, changing the paper sheets on the tables where patients were examined and taught their exercises, or helping patients from one exercise machine to another, wiping off the equipment and stuff.

One of the patients was a tall woman with red hair who had had a stroke. She walked with a cane because one of her legs didn't move right, and her arm looked stiff on that side of her body. Even one side of her face looked stiff. I had the strange feeling when I walked her back to the front desk that it was my mom I was helping, and I told Gwen about it later when we ate lunch in the cafeteria.

"Don't you remember *any*thing about your mom except that she was tall and had red hair?" Gwen asked, after she'd listened.

"She wore slacks a lot and she liked to sing, Lester told me once. And she always made Dad a pineapple upside-down cake for his birthday. And she was a good swimmer. All I've got are bits and pieces, and those all come from somebody else. I mean, I had her for five years, Gwen, and yet I hardly remember any of them."

"My aunt says you don't remember anything that happens to you before the age of four," Gwen said. "She says you could be scared by a man in a tall hat and you'd never remember it, but you'd go on being scared by men or tall hats and never know why."

"I guess that's why I want to be a psychiatrist," I said. "Find out what happened to me during those first four years."

Gwen wrinkled her nose. "Find out why you're as nutty as you are?"

"Exactly."

When I got home that day there was a little package waiting for me inside the screen. CARE PACKAGE, it said on the outside. Inside was a Hershey's bar, a paperback novel, a cassette, and a little notebook and pencil. FROM JILL AND KAREN, read the note. TO HELP YOU THROUGH THE REST OF THE WEEK.

That's what's so nice about friends.

Patrick had been calling every night, of course. "We *still* can't sit out on your porch?" he complained.

"We *especially* can't sit out on my porch," I told him. "Anything really fun or pleasurable is verboten."

Just after dinner, though, about the time the gang would be gathering to do something together, I heard someone call my name and went to the front door. Patrick and Pamela and Mark and Brian were all standing out by the street on the sidewalk.

"It's public property!" Pamela declared. "He can't drive us off."

Then Elizabeth came over. I sat on the swing on the porch and rocked, and we called back and forth, and pretty soon Elizabeth went home and came back with a ball of twine. Brian tied one end of it to a telephone pole, then threw the ball to me.

"Cable car!" he yelled. "Cable car."

While I watched, he took off one of his sneakers and tied the laces together over the line of the string. Patrick wrote a little note and dropped it in the sneaker. I came down off the porch and held the ball of twine taut to the ground, so that it tilted toward me, and Brian's sneaker came hurtling down. I read the note:

SO NEAR, AND YET SO FAR, Patrick had written. I laughed. I got a pencil from the house and on the other side of the note I wrote, YOU COULD ALWAYS CRAWL IN MY WINDOW. After I dropped it in the sneaker, I stood up on the porch and held the ball of twine high over my head, so that the sneaker went careening back the other way.

Patrick, the dope, read my note out loud, and the guys all whistled. I think I was having more fun being grounded than I was before. Dad came to the door once and looked out, but he didn't say anything.

Then the kids started sending me stuff in the shoe. Elizabeth went home again and came back with an all-day sucker. After that was delivered to me, I picked a bunch of Dad's asters growing by the steps and sent the bouquet back out to her.

We sent sticks and stones, nickels and dimes. I got a can of soda from the house and sent that, too. Somebody came by with a half-eaten ice-cream cone and even put that in Brian's sneaker, but it tipped over, and Brian had to wash out his shoe.

We had a great time.

That night Dad said, "I don't think I'm exactly getting through to you, am I, Al?"

"What do you mean?" I asked, knowing perfectly well what he meant.

"It's all fun and games to you, isn't it?"

"When your dad hands you a lemon, make lemonade," I said, paraphrasing Aunt Sally or somebody.

I think Dad almost smiled, but I wasn't sure. The thing was, Dad and I seemed to be growing a little apart, and it bothered me. On the one hand, I wanted to hug him, have things like they used to be between us, and wished I never had to leave home. On the other hand, I knew I had to leave someday, and I was sort of starting that slow separation now so that when it was time to make it official, I'd be ready.

Lester was having his problems, too. He left home that night at eight to go pick up Eva, but was back ten minutes later to shave again. I couldn't believe it. I thought he looked fine when he left here the first time, and I'll bet she asked him to shave again. "Maybe you should change your shoes, too, while you're at it," I joked.

"Shut up, Al," was all he said.

What a crazy, mixed-up summer it was.

I talked to the gang almost every day. Pamela and her dad were still arguing a lot, but at least she wasn't running away. All Elizabeth talked about was calories. She was getting so boring! Jill had been flirting with Justin Collier while Elizabeth was on her diet kick, and Patrick said he missed me.

I didn't want to sound too eager about the two weeks in August when Dad would be away—as though I were actually suggesting something—but the next time Patrick called and said he'd be glad when my punishment was up, I casually mentioned the fact that Lester and I would be by ourselves the last two weeks of August.

"No kidding!" said Patrick. "That's when I'll be in Maine with my folks."

I thought he must be joking. I was sure I'd told him before that Dad was going to England. "Not the whole two weeks!" I said.

"Two and a half, actually," he said. "It's some resort in Bar Harbor. We're getting together with my uncle and his family."

"Oh, Patrick!" I said.

There was a pause.

"It's only for two and a half weeks. It's not like I'll be gone forever," he said.

"But . . . but . . . " How could I say we could have been alone, on the porch, for two weeks? What I *really* meant was that we could try things— well, *he* maybe could try things—we hadn't done before, don't ask me what. But how would *that* sound? "I just . . . well, we wouldn't have Dad watching us all the time," I finished weakly.

Patrick only laughed.

After I hung up, I felt like a fool and sat staring at the wall. It was as though Aunt Sally had known exactly what was going through my head and had talked to God about it, and God had arranged for Patrick to be in Maine the two weeks I'd be most vulnerable. I could get around Dad, possibly, and Aunt Sally, too, but not Dad and Aunt Sally and God!

"This is the crummiest summer ever!" I told Lester when he came home that afternoon from the shoe store. He only grunted. He hadn't been in exactly the best mood either these days.

When I went to the Melody Inn again on Saturday to put in my three hours, Marilyn Rawley asked about Lester. She runs the Gift Shoppe three days a week after her classes at the university, and all day on Saturdays. She works even longer hours during the summer. On this particular morning she was wearing a thin cotton dress with little flowers on it, and sandals, and her long hair was pulled up off the back of her neck and tied with a ribbon.

"Hi, Alice," she said. "How's Lester?" And then, without missing a beat, she asked, "How's Eva?"

I looked at her. "How did you know about Eva?"

She smiled a little. "Word gets around. I hear she's really classy."

I wrinkled my nose the way Gwen does and tried to think of an appropriate answer while still being loyal to Lester. After all, he might marry Eva someday. "She's not you," I said.

"Well, of course she's not me, but what does that have to do with anything?"

"I don't know," I said. "I don't know about anything, and the world is all mixed up."

"Well, it doesn't get any better," Marilyn said, straightening the Brahms paperweights behind her, then rearranging the rack of Beethoven ties. "I told myself I'd get over Lester, and I'm not even close. I think about him, dream about him, cry about him . . . "

"What *is* it about my brother?" I asked, puzzled. "Crystal's married and she says *she* still dreams about him. I don't get it. I see him every day and I can't figure it out."

"He was tender, considerate, loving, romantic . . ."

"*Lester?*" I bleated. I mean, I *live* with him. I watch him eat breakfast when he's half asleep. I listen to him belch. I even wash his socks sometimes. But I guess when you love someone, it's not just when they're dressed in a suit and tie and wearing Brut aftershave . . . It's all the other times, too, when they're sick or smelly or grumpy or unreasonable . . .

"Well, I don't think Eva's good for him, if you want the truth," I told Marilyn.

"Lester never knew what was good for him," Marilyn agreed. And then, "I was the best thing that ever happened to him, and he let me go."

"He's inexplicable," I said, using a word I'd learned in English last semester.

We had my "coming-out" party the next day. It had been a week since I'd been grounded, and when I got to Mark Stedmeister's house that afternoon, everyone was there. Patrick gave me a long, slow kiss right in front of everyone, and they all clapped and cheered. Karen had even brought a cake that said WELCOME BACK! I almost wished I'd get grounded more often. Everybody was great, and said how much they'd missed me, and treated me as though this huge injustice had been done. I *still* thought my punishment was unfair, but Dad had made his point: I had assumed that Pamela's way was the *only* way to handle the situation. I didn't use my head. But that aside, I was prepared to enjoy my party. We laughed and splashed and sunned and loafed.

I was really surprised at Elizabeth, though—how much thinner she looked. I mean, we'd only been on our grooming kick for a month or so, and she had really slimmed down. In fact, she was beginning to look too bony in places.

She didn't eat any of the cake, I noticed, and when Mark's Mom brought out a pizza, Elizabeth didn't take any of that, either. I put a slice on a paper plate and set it in front of her, but she just broke off a corner of the crust and ate that. Every time I looked her way, she'd reach out and pretend she was going to take another bite. She'd hold it up to her lips and give the appearance of eating, but then she'd laugh and say something to someone and put it down again, or slide it from one side of her plate to another and never eat it at all.

"Hey, Elizabeth, you look great!" I told her. "You can eat again, you know."

"I'm eating!" she said, and ate another crumb.

We all debated whether to stick around at Mark's or go to a movie. His mom headed off to the mall, and we could have gone there, but didn't want to keep running into her. So we thought about going to the movies instead.

We were standing at the side of the pool drying off when I happened to look over at Elizabeth and see a long trickle of watery red running down the inside of her thigh. She was laughing and joking with Mark and Brian and hadn't even realized she'd started her period.

Pamela and I both saw it about the same time. We each sprang together, enveloping Elizabeth in our towels and moving her on toward the house. I think the guys had noticed, too, though, because I saw them nudge each other.

"What's the matter?" Elizabeth asked, confused. "What did I do?" That's Elizabeth for you. She automatically assumes she's guilty of something.

"I think you've started your period," I whispered when we were safely through Mark's back door and heading toward the basement bathroom.

Elizabeth came to a dead stop. "What?"

"It was sort of running down your leg," said Pamela.

"What?"

She yanked the towels away and saw pink smudges on them. "Oh, no!" She flung herself into the bathroom. "I'll never come out as long as I live!" she wailed plaintively "Anybody got any Kotex?"

"I don't," I said. "Just fold up some toilet

paper, Elizabeth, and tuck it in your pants."

"There isn't any! The roll's empty," Elizabeth bleated, "and I'm really menstruating hard now. Oh, my gosh!"

I don't know how so many things happen to Elizabeth. "I'll go get some from Mrs. Stedmeister," I said, and then remembered she was on her way to the mall. "Well, from Mark, then."

"No!" Elizabeth screeched from the other side of the bathroom door. "Don't you dare! I don't want him to know I'm walking around with toilet paper stuck in my pants."

She was absolutely impossible. Pamela went out on the deck and got her own bag. When she came back, she called, "Okay, Elizabeth, open the door. I've got something for you."

The bathroom door opened a crack. "What is it?" Elizabeth asked.

"A tampon."

Elizabeth looked at us in horror. "I can't! I'm a virgin!"

We stared at her.

"Hey, Elizabeth, we're virgins, too," I said, speaking for myself, at least. I'm never too sure about Pamela. "We can still use the junior size."

"No!" she cried just as Mark and Brian came in from outside. Elizabeth shut the door again. Pamela and I sat down on the floor in the hall to wait.

Brian studied us. "Where *is* everybody?" he asked.

"We're just waiting for Elizabeth," I told him.

The guys looked at us, then at the bathroom door, and finally turned and went back outside.

"Elizabeth, they're beginning to wonder," I called.

Elizabeth opened the door a crack. "I am not using a tampon!" she insisted. "I want to be a virgin on my wedding night."

Now Patrick stuck his head in the back door. "Hey, Alice! You going to get dressed?"

"When we get Elizabeth out of the bathroom," I said.

"What's taking so long?" he wanted to know.

"Feminine problems," said Pamela.

Patrick immediately disappeared.

Pamela pushed the tampon through the crack under the door.

"I won't use it!" said Elizabeth. "I'm just going to put my clothes back on and run home."

"Your clothes are still out by the pool, and we're not getting them for you until you put in that tampon," said Pamela. "Don't be such a dweeb."

Elizabeth began to wail.

"Elizabeth, shut up!" I whispered through the door. "They make tampons precisely for girls like us. Just gently insert the tampon and come out!"

Jill and Karen came in from outside.

"What's happening?" asked Karen.

"Elizabeth's in there losing her virginity," said Pamela.

"What?" gasped Karen.

"Tampons," I told them. "She's never used one before."

There was silence from the bathroom. Then Elizabeth's faint voice. "Do I take the paper off first or what?"

We all looked at each other.

"Take off the paper and insert it," ordered Pamela, her mouth to the door.

"Which end?"

"Not the end with the string, for heaven's sake. You have to pull it out again, remember," I said.

"It won't go in," Elizabeth whimpered. "It just goes halfway and stops."

Mark and Brian opened the back door and peered cautiously inside.

"Push, Elizabeth, push!" Karen was saying.

"Is she having a baby?" Mark joked.

"Elizabeth, will you hurry? They think you're in labor," I called as the boys went out again.

There was silence, and at last the door opened. Elizabeth was holding the empty cylinder in her hand and her forehead was wet with perspiration. But she had the triumphant look on her face of a woman who has conquered the universe.

10

Blue Monday

Dad says if I want to be a psychiatrist I have to go to medical school and become an MD first. *Then* I specialize in psychiatry.

"Why do I have to know about feet and intestines to understand why people act like they do?" I asked him.

"Because the body and mind work together. If you want to work in a hospital setting and be able to write prescriptions, you'd have to be a doctor," he told me. "But if you want to work in a clinic and see less seriously ill patients, you could probably be a psychologist. Get a Ph.D. And if you want to help people with common everyday problems who don't need long-term therapy, you could just get a master's degree and be a school counselor."

"How many years of college is that?"

"At least five."

"And I wouldn't have to dissect frogs' stomachs or pigs' lungs to graduate?"

"I doubt it," said Dad.

It was nice to know I had all those choices, provided I'm still interested in peoples' minds when I get to college. I was pretty sure I didn't want to work with their bodies. I liked to go in patients' rooms at the hospital and take them cards or flowers, see their faces light up, and sit and talk with them. But I didn't like to see them in pain. Didn't like to go into a room to find someone throwing up.

Gwen was definitely better at this than I was. She didn't see hospitals as depressing places at all. She saw them as hopeful.

"At least the people who work here are trying to make folks better," she said. "No one's trying to hurt them or make them worse."

When I got on the hospital elevator the first Wednesday in August, I heard a nurse address a man as "Mr. Plotkin." So that was my sixth-grade teacher's husband!

"Is Mrs. Plotkin here again?" I asked him.

He looked at me, and then smiled. "You must be Alice," he said. "Yes, I'm afraid so. She's been having quite a time with it. If we could just find the right combination of medicines . . . "

"Is she well enough for me to visit her?" I asked.

"Absolutely. She'd love to see you. Room 517

this time. I'm going home to attend to a few things, but I'll come back this evening."

I did all my assigned jobs first, then went up to fifth and entered her room. She looked a little fatter than I'd seen her last—well, puffy, maybe— but her skin was paler. Her smile was just as wide, though.

"Oh, Alice! Just the sunshine I was hoping for today," she said when she saw me.

I looked toward the window because it had been a foggy morning with no sun at all, but then I realized she meant me.

"Your heart again?" I asked, pulling a chair up to her bed.

"Oh . . . heart . . . kidneys . . . if it's not one thing, it's another. The trouble with medicine today, dear, is that what's good for one part of your body may be bad for another. But how are *you?* How's your summer going?"

"Sort of nuts, if you want the truth," I said. "Pamela's been fighting with her dad, Elizabeth's starving herself, Patrick's going to Maine for two and a half weeks, my dad's going to be away for two weeks . . . Everything's changing."

"Exactly," she said. "Because if it didn't, it wouldn't be life at all. No two days are ever alike."

I leaned forward, resting my elbows on my knees. "If you could go back to being any age you want, though, what would you choose?" I asked her.

Mrs. Plotkin laughed. "What makes you think I'd want to go back at all? I might choose to be the very age I am now, without all this hospital business, of course."

"You wouldn't want to be young again?" I asked, which seemed rude when I said it, but she didn't seem offended.

"A child, you mean? Well, a lot of that I've simply forgotten. My teenage years? Oh, I don't think so. They're such a roller coaster, you know. The twenties were exciting because I was starting out on my own; my thirties because I fell in love; my forties because I loved teaching so much and found I was good at it; my fifties because we did a lot of traveling; and my sixties . . . well, I haven't been sixty long enough to know, but I bet they'll be something. There's always hidden treasure waiting to be discovered."

I wasn't so sure about that, but I promised I'd come to see her again on Friday, and I told myself that this time I'd wear the ring she'd given me back in sixth grade, the one that used to belong to her great-grandmother. I wanted her to know I still had it.

At lunchtime I told Gwen about it, how Mrs. Plotkin wouldn't go back in time to choose her favorite year. Only I didn't say her name. I just said a favorite teacher of mine.

"She sounds exactly like my grandparents," said Gwen. "They always expect the *next* year to be their best, even in their seventies."

"Why not?" I asked. "Seventy years ago they hardly had any of the things we have now. Could hardly *do* any of the things we can do now."

"You can say that again," said Gwen, taking another bite of her egg salad sandwich. "Seventy years ago, girl, we wouldn't be sitting here together like this. *Forty* years ago, even, when my folks were little."

I keep forgetting. I guess I'm color-blind when it comes to Gwen.

"Do they ever talk about what it was like then, your grandparents?"

"All the time. And they tell me how much better I've got it. The problem is, the better I've got it, the more they expect of me. In my grandparents' time, for a black to graduate from college was really something. In my parents' time, you'd better go to college 'cause you had a lot to prove. And *my* generation—my folks wouldn't even *listen* if I said I wasn't going. If I said I just wanted to work at KMart or something, they'd say, '*What part of* no *don't you understand, girl?*'"

We laughed.

•   •   •

When I got home from the hospital and was reading the comics on the sofa, I got a call from Mrs. Price, Elizabeth's mother.

"Alice," she said. "I wonder if you could come over for a few minutes. Is this a bad time?"

"No, it's okay. I'll be over," I said. I knew that Elizabeth was at her piano lesson, and figured Mrs. Price needed to run to the store for something and wanted me to watch Nathan.

I slipped on my sandals and went across the street. Mrs. Price was wearing a backless sundress the color of grass, and had Nathan in her arms.

"I'm just getting ready to put him down for a nap," she said as he grinned at me and held out half his slimy graham cracker. "Be back in a minute. Sit down, Alice."

I went in the living room—the room with a huge photograph of Elizabeth in her first communion dress above the couch. I could hear Mrs. Price's footsteps on the floor above, Nathan's sleepy whine as she left his room, and soon she was back. Mrs. Price sat down across from me and smiled. She has dark hair and eyes, just like Elizabeth.

"How's the volunteer work going?" she asked. "Elizabeth tells me you're working at the hospital."

"It's okay," I told her. "I'd never want to be a doctor, though."

"Me either," she said. "The only time I've been

in a hospital overnight is when I had my children. Listen, would you like a Coke or something? Lemonade?"

What was this, I wondered? A tea party?

"No, I'm fine," I said.

She nodded. "Alice, I wanted to talk with you because I know you're probably Elizabeth's closest friend. You and Pamela, anyway. But I'd like this conversation to be confidential. I mean, I'd rather you didn't tell Elizabeth that we talked." She waited.

"Okay," I said, but I didn't feel good about it, because I didn't know what she was going to say next.

"How do you think she's looking lately?" her mother asked.

"Great! Elizabeth always looks great."

Mrs. Price smiled a little. "I meant . . . well, I know that you and Pamela and Elizabeth have been concentrating a lot on your clothes and looks this summer, and . . . well, I'm concerned about Elizabeth, frankly. I think maybe she's taking this weight business too far, and I wondered what you thought."

"I think she looks almost perfect right now," I said. "Except that her shoulders are beginning to look a little bony. She'd probably look better if she gained a few pounds, but she doesn't pay much attention to what I say. What I do know is that she wouldn't look good if she lost any more."

"I'm so glad you said that," Mrs. Price said. "I was afraid maybe you girls had agreed to lose a certain number of pounds this summer—a competition or something. Because I just don't like what I'm seeing in Elizabeth at all. If she eats, I don't know what. A bite here, a bite there . . ."

"I guess I figured she eats as little as she does when she's out with us because she eats more here," I said.

"And I figured it was just the other way around," said her mother. "That maybe she was filling up on junk food when she's out with her friends. To tell the truth, Alice, I'm scared to death she's going to be anorexic or something. When Elizabeth sets her mind to something, she's awfully hard to stop. I just wanted to be sure that you and Pamela weren't encouraging her to be so thin."

"Not me," I said. "One of the reasons we run in the mornings is so we *can* eat what we want. I do, anyway."

"Well, I really appreciate your coming over," she said. "I'm just not sure how to handle this, because I know that you're not supposed to nag."

"I'll do anything I can," I promised, getting up.

"Thanks, Alice. I know you will. You've been such a good friend to Elizabeth the last few years.

We were so happy when your family moved in across the street."

As I walked back home I wondered what was happening to us—Elizabeth and Pamela and me. Maybe fourteen was the year of the plagues. Maybe we were being punished for trying to make ourselves beautiful.

"Lester," I said at dinner, "if there was only one feature about me you could change, what would it be?" I knew better than to ask for a whole list.

"Your brain," he said, never taking his eyes off the sports page.

"*Visible*," I said. "Appearance-wise only."

"Your mouth," he said, and went on reading.

I knew it! I'd always supposed my lips were too thin. Maybe I'd have to get a collagen injection to make me look pouty. I tried to see my reflection in the glass door of the oven. "It's my lips, isn't it? They're too thin. Maybe I should have them enlarged."

"No, you should staple them shut," he said. "I'm trying to read the baseball scores."

I looked over at Dad.

"Al, you look perfectly fine to me. You look more like your mother every day, and I wouldn't change a thing," he told me.

Sometimes what he says is exactly right.

• • •

The next morning when Pamela and Elizabeth and I were running together, Pamela said, "I don't want to lose any weight; I just want to firm up my arms and thighs."

"Me either," I said. "I just want to stay healthy."

Elizabeth didn't say anything, just kept huffing away as we climbed the slope on the final leg of our run. So I added, hoping to appeal to her Catholic upbringing, "If I decide to marry and have children, I figure it's my moral responsibility to be strong and well-nourished." I was about as subtle as a jackhammer.

Elizabeth still didn't say anything, but Pamela looked at me in disbelief. "Who are you? Mother Teresa?"

"I'm just looking ahead," I said.

I noticed it didn't have much effect on Elizabeth, though, when the gang got together that night. Pamela had relaxed the no ice cream rule, because one of the things we like to do is walk over for ice cream, especially now that the shop has become a Baskin-Robbins. Elizabeth got real talky, the way she does when she wants to hide the fact that she's not eating. When the rest of us got our cones and she still hadn't ordered, I said, "Elizabeth, what kind are you getting?"

· "Oh . . . yeah," she said, and then, to the girl behind the counter, "one scoop of raspberry sherbet." She ate only a couple of bites, though, and threw the rest away when she thought no one was looking.

Actually, we had all noticed the girl behind the counter because she was new, she was petite, and she was cute. I'll bet she was a size three, with short dark curly hair and deep dimples in each cheek. She was also a well-developed three, nicely rounded, nothing skinny about her. But she was funny and bubbly, and the guys were kidding her about what year she graduated from kindergarten and did she still wear training pants. She seemed to enjoy the attention. I felt like an awkward elephant in comparison. Her name tag said PENNY.

Mark had given her a hard time. He'd asked for chocolate and she'd no sooner put her scoop in that container than he'd said, "Uh, no, make that pistachio." As soon as she reached for that, he'd said, "No, make it buttered almond," and so on. Finally she had just packed a little of each into a cone and handed it to him and he'd paid.

Brian found out she'd moved here in June and had been hired just a week ago. "I am *definitely* interested," he said about her as we sauntered home. "I *love* those curves!"

"Personality and pizzazz!" said Patrick.

I hoped Elizabeth heard. She only changed the subject.

I wore the ring with the big green stone in it to the hospital on Friday, and the first chance I got, looked at the patient register to see if Mrs. Plotkin was still there. She was. I wished I'd brought her something.

"Hi," I said, going in to sit next to her bed, then realized she'd been asleep, and I apologized all over the place for waking her.

"Oh, never mind that," she said. "I've got all day and all night to sleep. Not much else to do around here." I was noticing how gray her hair was now.

"Look," I said, holding out my hand with her great-grandmother's ring on it. It was still taped at the back so it would fit my finger.

"Oh, my goodness! You still have it. Now isn't that nice!" she said, smiling at me, and took my hand in hers, turning it this way and that so she could see the ring better. "I'm so glad I gave it to you, dear. It almost matches your eyes exactly."

"I'll keep it always," I told her.

"It was supposed to go to my daughter, you know. Those were my great-grandmother's instructions. Except that I had no children, so that settled that. Never had any nieces, either." She gave my hand a pat, as if to put an end to the conversation. "Now. How's the summer going?"

"About the same. Except Elizabeth's mom is worried about her because Elizabeth's so concerned about her weight."

"Wasn't she the pretty girl with the dark hair and fair skin? I think she was in someone else's class."

"That's the one," I said. "She had Mr. Weber."

"Oh, yes." Mrs. Plotkin closed her eyes for a moment and shook her head slightly. "It always amazes me," she said, "how some of the most beautiful girls are the most worried about their faces and figures. Why, look at the rest of us! The *ordinary* women. *We* got along all right, didn't we? We married, had careers . . . All this concern over beauty!"

Her voice drifted off, and I knew for sure I had interrupted her nap and shouldn't be there.

"I think I interrupted your nap," I said aloud. "Besides, I need to get down to the volunteer desk and see what they want me to do."

She smiled at me. "You're so sweet to drop in like this, dear. I always wonder what my students do once they leave my classroom, and you're one of the few who keeps in touch." She patted my hand again. "Make every day special, Alice. Each one *is* special, you know. Find something every day to be glad about." She winked. "And tell Elizabeth I said so."

I smiled, too, and then, on impulse, I leaned down and kissed her cheek. "Have a good nap," I said, and she smiled again and closed her eyes.

Gwen and I talked about her at lunchtime.

"When I first saw her at the start of sixth grade," I said, "I honestly thought she was the ugliest woman I'd ever seen. Her face . . . her nose . . . her receding chin and buck teeth . . . I did everything I could think of to get kicked out of her room so I could be in beautiful Miss Cole's classroom, but it didn't work. And by the time I left sixth grade, I loved her more than any other teacher I'd ever had. It was as though she'd changed—physically, I mean. She just wasn't ugly to me anymore, but *I* was the one who was changing."

"I've got an uncle like that. 'Uncle Ugly,' we used to call him, but he was so much fun, it just sort of turned into 'Uggie' and that's what we called him," Gwen said. "Uncle Uggie. The smallest cousins never did know how Uncle Albert got his nickname. Didn't even know what it stood for. But he wasn't ugly to me anymore, either."

I swirled the ice around in my cup and thought some more about my favorite teacher. "She said to make every day special."

"She got that right," said Gwen.

• • •

Patrick and I went to a movie over that Friday night. It was rated PG, but there was a real sexy scene in it—a woman in a black slip lying on top of a man, kissing him—and afterward, walking home, we stopped under some trees, and Patrick French-kissed me, putting his tongue all the way into my mouth, pushing it hard between my teeth, and I liked it. Liked the tight way he held me to him.

We were leaning against the trunk of a tree, and Patrick put his lips against my neck. "I go too far?" he asked.

"Huh-uh," I murmured, actually wishing he'd do it again, and he did. We stood with our arms around each other, and I said, "I wish you weren't going to Maine."

"So do I," he said.

Elizabeth invited Pamela and me for a sleep over Saturday night. She said her mom had suggested it, and I was sure of it when we were presented with hamburgers, pizza, and popcorn—the works. I guess Mrs. Price decided that if one thing didn't tempt Elizabeth, another might.

Elizabeth did eat half a hamburger, though she didn't touch the pizza. She also ate a few handfuls of popcorn and drank a couple sips of Coke. As we were getting ready for bed, though, she came into the room in her short pajamas, and Pamela exclaimed, "Gosh, Elizabeth, what's happening to your knees?"

"What?" Elizabeth said, freezing to the spot.

"*Look* at them!" Pamela said. "You're lost so much weight that your legs look like sticks and your kneecaps look huge."

Elizabeth broke into tears. I glared at Pamela, but it was too late. I'd never seen Elizabeth like this before. She suddenly picked up a piece of pizza off the pan and threw it at the window. *Elizabeth!*

"Hey, I'm sorry! I . . ." Pamela began.

Elizabeth threw another piece, and it splattered on the sill. We sat stunned, unable to say any more for fear she'd throw the whole pan.

"Justin thinks I'm too chubby! *You* think I'm too thin! I can't please *any*one!" she cried. She sat down on the bed, hands over her face, her shoulders shaking. I was scared out of my wits.

"Elizabeth, I'm really, really sorry!" Pamela kept saying. "I should have kept my big mouth shut."

In answer, Elizabeth suddenly grabbed the last piece of cold pizza and crammed the whole thing into her mouth at once—stuffing, stuffing—tomato sauce running down her chin, a piece of cheese glued to her cheek.

"'Ere!" she said, gulping it down. "Satisfied?" As

soon as there was any more room in her mouth, she grabbed a handful of popcorn and flattened it against her lips. And finally, after she'd swallowed, "I can't please *anyone*!" she repeated, tears streaming down her face. "Not you or Justin or Mom or Dad! Why do I even try?"

"Yes," I said, taking my cue. "Why *do* you?"

She wiped her mouth finally and sat breathing heavily, exhausted. "Why do I what?" she asked at last.

"Try to please everyone? Or *anyone*? What about you? What do *you* want?" *Dr. Alice, that's me.*

She only started crying again.

"Elizabeth, are you going to go your whole life trying to please other people instead of yourself?" I asked finally, still terrified inside.

She didn't even seem to be listening. "Nobody ever agrees!" she went on. "Mom says one thing, you say another . . ."

"Exactly," I said.

Elizabeth blew her nose, but she was still crying hard. "Nobody likes me just the way I am."

"Because we don't know *what* you are, Elizabeth, if you try to change all the time," Pamela said.

"You have to figure out the place where *you're* comfortable and happy and healthy and then stay there," I told her. "Never mind what anybody else says."

"Yeah, but how do I know—?"

Pamela cut in. "If you're always hungry and thinking about food, you're not healthy and you know it. Or if you're always eating every excuse you get and never letting yourself feel hungry, that's not good either."

"She's right," I said. "If *you* get to the place where you like yourself the way you are, Elizabeth, that's how others will like you, too."

We cleaned up the pizza mess, and Elizabeth went in the bathroom to wash her face. I heard the stairs creak below and knew that Mrs. Price had probably been down there trying to figure out what all the commotion was about. Afterward we turned on Elizabeth's TV and sat on her bed, finishing the popcorn. But every so often, Pamela and I glanced uncertainly at each other. Had we helped? Had we hurt? Elizabeth was the first friend we'd had who might be getting anorexic, and we felt as helpless as her mother did.

Monday was one of those wet, humid days in Maryland when it feels as though the Chesapeake Bay is floating just over your head and could dump on you at any moment. Everything you touched felt sticky, and there wasn't any breeze. It was a pleasure to step inside the hospital and feel the air-conditioning cool my arms and face.

Gwen and I signed in at the volunteers' desk and got our assignments for the day. I checked the patient register to see if Mrs. Plotkin was still there, and she was, so I was pleased I wasn't assigned to physical therapy all morning.

I was supposed to stock shelves in the gift shop and then do magazine rotation in all the waiting rooms. That means weeding out magazines that are more than a month old and replacing them with current issues. Gwen was on mail delivery, and we passed each other on fourth and took a few minutes to leaf through an old *People* magazine to see which stars were still married to whom.

I had just changed magazines in the waiting room of the maternity ward—leaving plenty of *Field and Stream, Sports Illustrated, Worth,* and *Newsweek* for expectant fathers and putting the old magazines back on my cart—when I heard a code blue.

Gwen had taught me to listen for that. This very calm but determined-sounding voice announces, "Code blue, code blue," and a room number, then a couple of doctors' names. What it means is that a patient is having a crisis—his heart has stopped or something—and that those doctors are to go immediately to that room.

I had just turned the corner with my cart when I heard, "Code blue 517, code blue 517, Doctors Roland and Garcia. Code blue, code blue . . ."

Mrs. Plotkin!

I left my cart and ran for the stairs. My heart pounding, mouth dry, I reached the floor above and opened the door to the corridor to see nurses and attendants gathering outside Mrs. Plotkin's room, pushing in a cart full of equipment. The elevator door opened, and a doctor hurried out and on down the corridor to 517.

I went down the hall as far as I dared, my back flat against the wall. I saw Mr. Plotkin come out, his face as white as chalk, a nurse with him, holding him by the arm.

More technicians. Another doctor. Voices. I couldn't move. The nurse walked Mr. Plotkin on down the hall in the other direction.

For a long time the people stayed in the room, and I stood unmoving in the hallway, like a potted plant.

And then, one by one, they began coming out. The cart with all the equipment came first, then one technician, then another. No one was hurrying anymore. Doctors stood outside the room talking in low voices, writing things on their charts.

When the nurse came back with Mr. Plotkin, one of the doctors put his arm around his shoulder. I closed my eyes and felt tears welling up under my eyelids.

"Alice?"

I opened them again to see Gwen.

"What's the matter?" she asked, looking at me strangely. "Mrs. Hensley sent me to look for you. One of the nurses reported a magazine cart left outside 409, and . . . "

I could only cry.

Gwen led me to the sunroom at the end of the corridor and sat me down on the wicker couch. She put an arm around me just as a doctor had done to Mr. Plotkin. I buried my face against her and bawled, and she put both arms around me and rocked.

"Was it her?" she guessed. "Your teacher?"

I nodded and only sobbed.

"Oh, girl, I'm so sorry," she said. "I'm sorry."

"I just saw her last Friday!" I wept. "I never knew . . . I never thought . . ."

"Girl . . . girl . . . girl . . .," Gwen soothed.

I sobbed all the harder and couldn't seem to stop. "I wore h-her ring," I wept. "And . . . and I even k-kissed her, but I never said what she really n-needed to hear, Gwen. That I loved her."

11

For Girls Only

I went to the funeral on Friday with Dad. Pamela had said she'd go with me, but changed her mind at the last minute. She doesn't like funerals, she said.

"Pamela, nobody goes because they *enjoy* it," I told her. "You go because it's your last chance to say good-bye."

"If I said it, she wouldn't hear me," Pamela said. "I hate funerals. I don't need anything else depressing in my life right now."

That much was true. But all week I'd felt this huge sadness. It was hard to explain. Not even Patrick understood. He wasn't going to the funeral, either, because of his drum lesson.

"She was a good teacher, but it's not like she was a relative or anything," he'd told me.

"To me, she was," I'd said, and immediately clouded up.

Dad didn't try to analyze it. He waited till I'd stuffed Kleenex in all my pockets, and then we drove to the Methodist Church for the memorial service. It was a beautiful summer day, a day we all should have been out enjoying the sun, but instead I was saying good-bye to the best teacher I ever had.

I don't know what I expected—a church packed with former students, I suppose; all the teachers from the elementary school. But there were only about a hundred people there, most of them in their fifties and sixties—neighbors of the Plotkins', I guess, and people from her church. The only person I recognized was the elementary school principal.

I wished I'd sent flowers. Why hadn't I bought a huge bouquet with a ribbon that read, TO MY BELOVED TEACHER? Why hadn't I called up everyone who had been in sixth grade with me and insisted they come to the service? Why hadn't I *dragged* Pamela, *shamed* Patrick into coming?

When we sat down, however, I realized that Mrs. Plotkin wasn't there. I looked around for a coffin, but saw only the two big bouquets of flowers on either side of the altar. I looked at Dad quizzically, and he understood.

"Many people don't have burials, Al," he whispered. "They want their bodies cremated or donated to science, and the family just holds a memorial service."

I nodded. I was relieved, I guess, because I wanted to remember her the way she was when she held my hand there in the hospital, and I kissed her. Remember the way she'd smile at me when I walked in her room, as though I were the person she wanted most to see in the whole world.

A man was playing the organ. I don't know why organ music is always so sad to me. But everyone was very quiet. The principal sat looking thoughtfully out a side window. Dad reached over and put his hand on mine. I liked having it there, as though it could protect me from all the sad things that happen in life, even though I knew it couldn't.

Mr. Plotkin came down the aisle with several other people—relatives, I suppose—and after they sat down in the front row, a minister in a black robe got up and read from the Bible—"The Lord is my shepherd . . ."—and then he said we had all come to share our memories of a fine woman and a wonderful friend.

Isn't it weird how you never imagine your teachers doing anything else but teaching school? I remember how, when I first found out that Mrs. Plotkin was married, I tried to imagine her in bed, making love to a man. I felt tears again and brushed them away.

The minister talked about what a faithful member of the church Mrs. Plotkin had been—a member of the welcoming committee, the committee on church and society, the worship committee, and, of course, the choir. What a beautiful voice she had had, the many times she had sung an alto solo. All news to me. Since she had retired after thirty years of teaching, she had helped cook at a homeless shelter, tutored inner-city children, helped two nephews through college, sponsored an orphaned child in India, and was a docent at the Children's Museum, he told us. Then he said that if any of us wanted to share with the others some memories of our own, we were welcome to do so at this time.

For a moment no one said anything. The minister simply sat down in a chair and waited. Then a man sitting beside Mr. Plotkin got up and said he was Mrs. Plotkin's brother, and how he'd had a hard time in high school with algebra, and how his sister had helped him through it. He was probably her first pupil, he said, and people smiled.

A woman near the back said that she was a neighbor of the Plotkins', and that whenever there was a crisis, any neighbor needing help, Mrs. Plotkin was the first one there. Several more people stood up and said nice things, and then there was another long silence.

This was all? My stomach tensed, my legs felt numb, my throat began to tighten up, but I knew I had to do this one last thing for Mrs. Plotkin. I let go of Dad's hand and shakily got to my feet. Like the others, I turned and faced the audience. It reminded me of the sixth-grade play in Mrs. Plotkin's room. I remembered how she had instructed us—those of us with speaking parts, of which I was not one—to speak up and enunciate clearly.

"I . . . I didn't know Mrs. Plotkin as long as the rest of you have," I stammered, "but I just want t-to say that she was probably the b-best teacher I ever had. She was kind to me even when I didn't deserve it, and it made me a better person. . . . "

There was so much more I could have said—*wanted* to say—but it would have taken an hour. So I just sat back down, and Dad put his arm around my shoulder and squeezed it. Mr. Plotkin looked back at me and smiled. Once again, the tears came.

The minister stood up finally and read something by Mr. Plotkin about how much he loved his wife, and all the happy years they'd had together. Then the organ was playing again, and the minister led the congregation in prayer.

It suddenly occurred to me that I had stood up in front of my father and said that Mrs. Plotkin was the best teacher I'd ever had. Not Miss Summers, the woman he loved. I felt my face beginning to turn red. And then I realized it was the truth. I loved Miss Summers; she'd been a wonderful teacher. But it was pear-shaped Mrs. Plotkin who sort of saved me from myself. Who taught me that beauty on the inside meant a whole lot more than skin and weight and hair and makeup. So what was I doing spending so much of the summer thinking about myself?

When the service was over, I had turned to leave with Dad when I felt someone clutch my arm. It was Mr. Plotkin. His face looked almost as gray as his suit, and the pouches beneath his eyes looked like little bags for carrying all the extra sadness that his head couldn't hold.

"Alice," he said, taking both my hands in his, "it was so nice of you to come. Thank you for what you said."

"I'll always remember her," I said, and showed him the ring she gave me.

"I know," he said. "She told me."

"I'm so sorry she's gone," I choked.

"I know," he said again.

I couldn't see, because my eyes were so blurred with tears. Dad put his arm around me once more, and we went back out to the car. All the way home, though, I cried. The more I cried, the more disgusted I felt Dad must be with me. It was as though I was telling him that Mrs. Plotkin meant more to me than Miss Summers ever had, but I couldn't help it. I cried in big gulping, gasping sobs, and when we got home, Dad parked the car in the driveway but didn't make any move to open the door.

"I . . . I'm sorry," I said at last, my face all scrunched up, puffy and feverish. "I don't know what's the matter with me. It's as though she were part of the family."

"I think she was, Al," Dad said quietly. "I think she came closest, maybe, to being a mother to you for a while. You never did, you know, get a chance to really grieve for your mom; you were too young to understand the finality of it. I think it's a fine thing that you loved Mrs. Plotkin so much. If you hadn't, you wouldn't miss her so much now."

Pamela came over that evening, but she didn't want to talk about funerals. We were both sitting around moping when Elizabeth called.

"Mom's got this surprise worked up, if you guys want to do it," she said.

What Mrs. Price had "worked up," in fact, were three tickets to an all-day seminar called "For Girls

Only." It would be held at the Y the following day, and she had got the last tickets left. There would be two sessions in the morning, a box lunch, and an afternoon session, all for girls between the ages of twelve and fifteen. A nurse would talk to us about our changing bodies, a nutritionist would talk to us about diet, and a fashion consultant would talk about grooming, which is a weird word, in my opinion. It always reminds me of horses.

"We'll probably be the oldest ones there, but let's do it," said Pamela, desperate for anything to pass the time.

"I'll go if you'll go," Elizabeth said.

"I'm sure Dad will let me off at the Melody Inn," I said.

So the next morning we let the running go, and took the bus to the Y.

"I hope they don't spend the whole time explaining menstruation," said Pamela.

"Mom said the emphasis was on looking good," said Elizabeth.

I hoped they wouldn't tell me my calves were too straight or my lips were too thin or that any other part of my body was out of line somehow. I didn't want to think that implants and liposuction were part of my future. I don't quite trust these grooming seminars.

We were glad to see that at least a third of the audience was our age. The room had salmon-colored walls, royal blue chairs, and photos all over the walls of interesting women and girls—news commentators, scientists, TV stars, athletes, artists, singers. . . . Some were fat, some were thin, some were young, some were old. FOR GIRLS ONLY, said a banner on the wall at the front of the room, and there were paper cups of orange juice and bowls of peanuts on the window ledge.

We sat around breaking open the peanuts and tossing the shells in the waste basket, asking each other what school they went to, getting acquainted.

The program director at the Y was a young woman in jeans and a polo shirt who welcomed us to the seminar.

"This is for girls only," she said, smiling, "so if there are any boys here in disguise . . . "

We laughed.

She went over the program with us, then introduced the fashion consultant. I was glad to see that she weighed more than ninety pounds, and didn't look as though she had been in a concentration camp for the last three years. Her hair was red—dyed, probably, but it looked good—and she was wearing a filmy green and gold summer dress with green sandals. She sat on a high stool and kept her knees together.

"The secret of looking good," she told us, "is to feel good about yourself. If you're comfortable with your body and your clothes, you can relax and concentrate on your friends and conversation. If you're worried about being too tall, however, you'll walk slouched over. If you think you're too fat, you'll be thinking about hiding your stomach. If you're uncomfortable about your appearance, you'll always be tugging at something, checking something, concealing something—and your friends will feel uneasy around you. The aim is to learn what looks best and feels best on you, how to dress and fix yourself up in the simplest way, and then forget about it."

That sure made sense to me. Then she gave us all kinds of tips for looking better: Pay attention to the colors your friends compliment you in; if you're short waisted and want to look longer from your shoulders to your waist, wear a belt the same color as your shirt. If you want to look *shorter* from your shoulders to your waist, wear a belt the same color as your skirt or pants . . .

Elizabeth, of course, was making notes, and Pamela and I figured we could just read what she'd written if we wanted to remember something. The consultant went on: A short, quick squirt of cologne is all you need, don't overdo; don't just brush your teeth, brush your tongue if you want to avoid bad breath; forget green and blue mascara, just accent the colors in your own skin . . .

Each of us got a color analysis and a few personal tips before the first session ended, and I was glad that the fashion consultant didn't frown or gag or anything when she looked me over. "Nice skin," she said. "Great eyes."

We lined up for more orange juice at the back of the room.

"Well, *that* was informative!" Elizabeth said enthusiastically. We were all trying to figure out if the fashion consultant wore any makeup at all or had applied it so skillfully that it looked completely natural.

"Makeup," said Pamela. "Definitely makeup. Nobody could look that good bare naked."

The second session was on nutrition, and I'd bet anything this was the reason Mrs. Price had bought tickets to the seminar. The nutritionist, though, was a young perky woman in shorts and a tee who talked about body build and the whole range of weights that went with each height.

"Just a few simple rules, girls, to keep your weight in the right range, and they really *are* simple," she told us. "You don't have to count calories. You don't have to weigh your food. Best of all, you don't have to give up *any*thing. First, if you know you're going to have a big meal or a special treat, go easy the rest of the day and do twenty minutes extra of vigorous exercise. It's a trade-off.

"Second: Don't eat when you're not hungry. Don't put anything in your mouth until you know you've got a stomach—till you can feel it talking to you. Then eat until you're reasonably satisfied, not stuffed, and stop.

"Third, fill up as much as possible on fruits and veggies. Eat all the fruit you want. Exercise every day, drink lots and lots of water, and then forget it. If you do all this, then whatever weight you are is the weight that's right for you."

After that, with a lot of giggling and moans and sighs, each girl was asked to step behind a little curtain—something like a voting booth—and get weighed and measured. Then she was given a slip of paper with her height and weight on it, and the right range of weights for her.

"Anything above this range is too heavy, girls. Anything below is too thin. But notice that there's twenty or so pounds here to play around with. No two girls are ever alike."

We had sliced chicken and avocado wraps in our box lunches, each with a bunch of grapes, carrot sticks, and oatmeal-raisin cookies. And all the lemonade we could drink.

Elizabeth and Pamela and I sat together and

compared our weight slips. The nutritionist said
we could keep them private if we liked, but Pamela
and I shared ours with each other. Pamela was
dead center, I was six pounds up from average,
and then, because Pamela and I had shown her
our slips, Elizabeth showed us hers: eight pounds
off the range on the low end.

"Well, you *do* want to get rid of those bony
knees, Elizabeth," said Pamela. "You'd look great
with another eight pounds."

Elizabeth was quiet for a while. "What if I can't
stop?" she asked finally.

"Stop what?" I wanted to know.

"Eating. What if I start putting on weight and
keep stuffing and stuffing . . ."

"You never had that problem before, so why
should you have it now?" Pamela asked.

And I said, "Just because Justin Collier made a
dumb remark, you're either going to starve yourself or go on a feeding frenzy? Don't give him that
power. *You* decide what goes in your mouth. Justin
should have no say in the matter."

Elizabeth didn't answer, but she *did* eat all her
lunch. All but the oatmeal cookies. Still, it was a
start.

It was the afternoon session, though, that blew
us away. The nutritionist took us for a walk around

the Y, and then turned us over to a nurse for the third session. When we came back to the room with the salmon-colored walls and the royal blue chairs, we gasped and giggled and stared, for there on the front wall—the whole length of the wall— were anatomically correct drawings of nude boys. Fat boys, thin boys, tall boys, short boys, front and back.

We all began laughing and clapping, and the nurse—a plumpish thirtyish woman—laughed, too.

"Enjoy!" she said.

Even Elizabeth laughed. We gathered at the front of the room and gaped at the drawings. Every boy had a penis, of course, and no two penises were exactly alike. Some were long and thin, some were short and thick. Small and thick, long and thick, circumcised, uncircumcised, big testicles, small testicles . . . Some of the boys had no hair on their bodies at all, and some had hair all over their backs and abdomens. Some of the boys, in fact, had puffy breasts that almost looked like a girl's. Skinny legs, thick legs, bowlegs, short legs . . . I don't think any of us realized that boys were so different under their jeans.

"Now," said the nurse. Smiling mysteriously, she went over to the door and pulled down the shade. "Are you ready?"

We looked at her uneasily. She went to the front of the room and unfastened the long poster of the naked boys, and this time we began to squirm and shriek, because there, underneath, was a long poster of naked girls, front and back. Not just naked, either. Some were bending over, some were sitting with their legs apart, some were standing.

Elizabeth, her face red with embarrassment, half rose from her seat as though to leave the room, but the nurse, laughing, stopped her.

"Right now," she said, "I think all of us are squirming a bit. In a way, we'd all like to leave this room, because these are parts of female bodies you just don't see without making a special effort. From the time they are babies, boys can examine themselves and look at each other and see immediately what they've got. But did you know, girls, that some women get married, have babies, and become grandmothers, even, and they never know what they really look like down there?"

I don't think it was anything I'd thought about consciously, but I knew it was true. How *could* I see what I looked like without almost standing on my head?

"Relax," the nurse told us. "We're not going to undress and I'm not going to examine you. But before you leave today, I want you to at least know the names of your most intimate body parts, and where they're located."

She flipped back a large sheet of paper on the huge easel at the front of the room, and there was a big drawing of a woman's privates more detailed than anything we'd ever seen in health and hygiene class.

"The pubis," the nurse said, pointing to the bulge of fat covered with hair between a woman's legs and, pointing to the two sides of the vaginal opening, said, "The vulva. These outer sides, or lips, are called the labia majora, and the inner lips are called the labia minora." Her pointer touched a little pea-sized lump at the top end of the opening. "This is the clitoris—the little button where your most intense sexual feelings are located. The urinary opening, or urethra, is right under that, not easy at all to see, and the opening under *that* is the vagina. See this little fold of skin over part of the vagina? That's the hymen. And back here is the anus; the space between the vagina and the anus is called the perineum. You would be surprised at the number of women who don't know where the urine comes out. Or where exactly the vagina is located. Or the number of women who think sexual excitement has something to do with urinating, because everything is so close together down there."

We didn't move. I wondered if some of us were even breathing. We didn't look to the left or the right.

The nurse faced us. "Okay, this is serious, now. You've seen the pictures of boys. If you didn't know before, you know now that all boys are different. They come in all sizes and shapes, with all sorts of variations in their sexual equipment. And every one of those boys is perfectly normal. You girls are the same way. We come in all sizes and shapes, with loads of variations."

We stared at the long poster stretched across the front of the room, with all different kinds of intimate parts exposed. The nurse lifted her pointer again. "Now," she said, "if you leave here today with no other memory of anything I've told you, I want you to remember this: We are all normal." She began moving the pointer down the row of pictures. "Some girls have breasts the size of grapefruit: normal. Some have breasts the size of lemons: normal. Some have breasts the size of pecans . . ." We laughed. "Normal," she said. "Perfectly normal.

"Some girls are as flat as two fried eggs: normal. Some girls have belly buttons that sink in: normal. Some have 'outies': normal. Some have fine body hair on their thighs or abdomens or between their breasts: normal. Some have big nipples: normal.

Some have small nipples: normal. Some have labia minora all tucked up inside where you can hardly see them: normal. Some have labia minora that protrude from between their outer lips: normal. Some have a clitoris so small, you can hardly see it: normal. Some have a clitoris an inch long: normal. Some have a hymen almost covering the vagina: normal. Some girls, even virgins, have practically no hymen at all: normal. Some have buttocks that rise high and stick out: normal. Some have flat buttocks: normal. How ever you are built, girls, your body is normal."

She walked along beneath the poster, touching each girl's picture in turn. "Normal, normal, normal, normal, normal . . ."

It was the most welcome news I had heard in a long time. All the little oddities about my body I'd wondered about had been pronounced normal.

"Now," said the nurse, smiling around the group. "That wasn't so hard, was it? I'm going to give you each an assignment, and I'll never know if you did it or not. It's entirely up to you. But sometime, when you're alone in your room or the bathroom, when you know you won't be disturbed, I want you to take a hand mirror and examine yourselves."

All of us gasped and giggled and covered our faces at the same time. We were all Elizabeths.

"It's not wrong, it's not silly, it's not sinful to want to know more about yourself," said the nurse. "It's sensible and healthy. I want you to be able to tell a doctor where there's a problem. I want you to be able to say, 'There's an irritation around my clitoris,' or 'a discharge from my vagina,' or 'a sore on my labia,' or 'a burning around my urethra.' When boys have a problem, they know right where it is. Why can't we? We're a long way, girls, from the women of Victorian times who wouldn't even take off their clothes when they went to a doctor. They'd just point to a place on a doll's body where they were having symptoms and the doctor was supposed to tell them what was wrong without ever examining them. Thank goodness we don't do *that* anymore, but we still have a long way to go."

When we got off the bus coming back from the Y, we walked slowly along the sidewalk, the nurse's words ringing in our ears: *normal, normal, normal, normal, normal . . .*

"Wow!" said Pamela finally. "I always wondered what I looked like down there. I tried to look at myself once with a mirror in the bathtub, but it seemed so obscene . . . "

I expected Elizabeth to say, "Pamela!" but she didn't. She didn't say anything at all.

"I never knew where my urethra was," I confessed. "I had no idea where the pee comes out. Just somewhere down there."

"But in *back* of the clitoris. Now that was news to me," said Pamela.

Elizabeth didn't even slow down, just kept walking.

"Boys know from the time they're one year old where the pee comes out," Pamela went on. "Everything on a boy is so accessible! I had a cousin once who told me he used to write his name in the snow with his pee."

Elizabeth stopped. "What?"

"He just took his hand and guided his penis, and spelled the word Bob," Pamela told her.

I laughed out loud.

"Now if you wanted to pee your name in the snow, Elizabeth," said Pamela, "you'd have to squat down and . . ."

"Shut up!" said Elizabeth, laughing.

"Well, we learned a lot today," Pamela continued. "At least on your wedding night, Elizabeth, you'll be able to tell your husband exactly where you want him to touch you. *Forward of the urethra, please, and then you can do the perineum . . .*"

"Stop it!" Elizabeth said again, but she was laughing even harder.

"I'm an inny," I offered.

"Outie," said Pamela.

"Inny, too," said Elizabeth.

We put our arms around each other as we walked three abreast.

"Well, I've got pecans," said Elizabeth after a minute.

"Lemons," I said.

"I've got *cantaloupes,"* Pamela bragged.

"Oh, Pamela, you do not!" we told her.

"Normal," she said.

"Normal," said Elizabeth.

"Normal," I repeated, and we moved on down the sidewalk in step, pondering the mysteries of womanhood.

12

The Next Good-bye

I was determined to do the nurse's assignment as soon as I got home, before I lost my nerve, but I couldn't find a hand mirror, not any that was big enough, and I didn't feel like asking Elizabeth for one. I felt really good, though. Isn't it weird how what a person says about you can affect how you feel about yourself? I'm the very same person I was before I went to the seminar where the nurse pronounced us normal, but I felt ten times better. Which helped me understand how awful Elizabeth had felt when Justin called her chubby.

Dad and Lester got home about the same time and were debating what to make for dinner, when I came downstairs.

"Do we have a hand mirror?" I asked from the kitchen doorway.

"Never use one," said Lester, examining the date on a carton of sour cream.

"Naturally, you're a male. What you see is what you've got," I said resentfully.

"Huh?" said Lester.

"I don't know whether we have one or not," said Dad. "There might be one in my bottom dresser drawer. It belonged to your mother. I *think* that's where I put it."

"If you want to see the back of your head, Al, don't bother. It's a rat's nest," said Lester.

"I don't," I said. "For your information, Lester, there are at least five wonderful parts of the female body that can be viewed by the owner only with a hand mirror." And as they stared after me, I went regally back down the hallway and up the stairs to Dad's room.

Just as Dad had said, there was an oval mirror with a blue handle beneath his pajamas in the bottom drawer. I carefully lifted it out and studied the white flowers painted on the back. I smiled to myself, wondering if Mom had ever used the mirror for self-inspection.

I went back in my bedroom and locked the door. I couldn't help laughing, though, because it still seemed a little embarrassing, even though I was the only one there. I peeled off my jeans and underpants, then lay back on the bed with the mirror propped between my knees, and a couple of pillows under my head.

It took a little adjusting and probing to see anything, but sure enough, there was my labia majora and, peeking out from between the lips, the labia minora. I pulled the lips apart and found the little pea-sized clitoris, so sensitive I could hardly touch it. I found my vagina all right, and maybe the hymen, and of course I recognized my anus, though I'm sure I never saw it before. What a weird feeling to think you were being introduced to parts of yourself you'd had for fourteen years and never yet laid eyes on. The urethra was the most difficult of all to find, but I think I even got that straight. The big surprise, though, was a light brown irregular shaped birthmark on my skin just to the left of my vulva.

Well, I said to my privates, *Nice to meet you.* I laughed again and thought how the nurse would have smiled, too, if she were here. I'll bet Pamela had already studied herself, inside and out. Elizabeth? I don't think so, but sometimes she'll surprise you.

I dressed, put the mirror back in Dad's drawer, and went downstairs. Dad and Lester had decided to make pesto sauce, and Les was heating the water to boil pasta. Neither of them looked at me when I came in and sat on the edge of the table, and I could swear I saw them blush.

"I just discovered the most amazing thing," I said.

"You're a hermaphrodite?" said Lester.

"What?"

"Half male, half female?"

"There *are* such people?" I asked, astonished.

"Sometimes nature makes a mistake, Al, but surgery can do wonderful things now," Dad told me. "So what did you discover about yourself?"

"I just discovered a birthmark I didn't know I had."

He *was* blushing a little. I had actually made my father blush. "Uh-huh," he said, and went on stirring.

"It's right beside my vulva on the left," I announced.

"Will you stop?" said Lester.

But Dad said, "Sort of a butterfly shape?"

Now *I* was blushing. "How did you know?"

"Honey, I *am* your father," he said. "I used to change your diapers, remember? No, of course you don't." Then he smiled. "Marie pointed it out to me when I held you in the hospital. She had already looked you over, every inch of you, and she said that if they ever sent us home with the wrong baby, we'd know because of that birthmark."

"Darn!" said Lester. "No matter how hard we try, we just can't get rid of her."

I fixed my attention on Lester. "I suppose even *you* changed my diaper?"

"Are you nuts?" he said. "I was only seven. I couldn't stand the smell of a diaper, much less the sight of one."

The phone rang just then, and Les answered, and then, "Hi, beautiful," he said. There was a pause. "Sure, I'm game. What's up?" There was an even longer pause. Finally he said, "I'll see what I can manage," and a minute later he hung up.

For the first time I'd heard some irritation in Lester's voice when he talked to Eva.

"Change of plans," he said to us. "I thought Eva and I were going to watch a video at her place, but she wants to go to Georgetown instead. 'Bring lots of money,' she says."

"What for?" I asked.

"Shopping. What else?"

I thought it over. "Well, if she wants to shop in Georgetown, why doesn't *she* bring the money?"

"Good point," Lester said, but didn't answer.

On Monday there was a big car show at Wheaton Plaza, and a whole bunch of kids from school were there, so we shoved some tables together at Wendy's and all ordered burgers and fries. I saw friends I hadn't seen since June. Gwen was there with her boyfriend, "Legs." He is the tallest, skinniest boy I've ever met, but there's nothing anorexic about him. He eats till you tell him to stop. Lori and Leslie were there, and also Sam and his girlfriend, the one he took to the eighth-grade formal after I'd turned him down.

Sam still liked me some, I knew, and I guess I sort of enjoyed knowing there was a potential boyfriend waiting in the wings, should anything happen between Patrick and me. But he liked his new girl friend, too, Jennifer, who had this wild mane of curly hair. They always had their arms around each other, but once in a while I'd catch him looking at me the way he used to in biology. We ate and joked and caught up on each other's news, and I thought, now *this* is the way summer is supposed to be.

And then on Tuesday, something happened so unexpected that I could hardly believe it. I came downstairs to go jogging with Elizabeth and Pamela, and when I met them outside, both were crying.

"What's wrong?" I asked.

Elizabeth turned to me. "Pamela's moving," she said.

"What?"

Pamela swallowed, but her voice was harsh and determined. "I'm going to live with Mom," she said. "Dad and I had the most awful argument last night. I called Mom, and she said she guessed I could live with them, and she's sending me a plane ticket for next week."

"Pamela!" It's all I could say.

We didn't run that morning. We sat out on my porch, and Pamela cried and talked, then cried and talked some more. Her dad insisted on knowing everything she did, she told us. Everyplace she went. Every person she saw.

"He says I'll end up like my mother," she wept. "He called me a tramp. He won't let me have any fun at all, and it'll only get worse when I'm in high school. I can't stand it any longer."

"But . . . where are you going to sleep? I thought your mom and her boyfriend were in a one-bedroom apartment in Colorado."

"They are, but Mom says they'll find a two-bedroom. It has to be better there, it just has to." Then she said, "What do I care? I don't have a boyfriend. Everything's so unsettled."

"You have us," I said. That only made her cry again.

When I found out the reservation had been made, though, and she was determined to go, I figured the least we could do for Pamela was help her pack and be as supportive as we could. But I still couldn't believe it. Elizabeth and Pamela and I had been together for a long time. Well, three years, anyway. We were best friends. Weren't we all going to go to the high school prom together when we got to be seniors? Hadn't we talked about going to the same college, maybe, and calling each other when we got engaged?

Elizabeth threw her arms around Pamela. "It wasn't supposed to be this way," she said.

Nothing is ever the way you thought it would be.

By late afternoon, when we gathered at Mark's, everyone had heard the news. Gwen and Legs had come over, too, and we all sat staring at Pamela. Mark and Brian, who'd both had crushes on her in the past, looked chagrined, as though they'd been counting on dating her again. Karen and Jill were stunned that she would even consider moving away. Patrick simply said she was nuts.

"You hardly even know this guy your mom's dating, Pamela. He could be a thousand times worse than your dad," he said.

"You got that right," said Legs, the only one of us who was eating pretzels while we digested the news. "Dad left us when I was six, and all I wanted was a father. Then I got this stepdad, and all I wanted was for him to leave. Best day of my life was the day he walked out."

Karen and Brian, who are both from single-parent homes, agreed, but I saw Gwen elbow Legs to keep him from saying more. "It'll be okay, Pamela," she said. "Think positive."

Pamela, though, appeared to be fighting back

tears, sitting there in her red bathing suit, running one hand over her knuckles distractedly. "Well, Mom said maybe I can work in their ski shop when they start one. I think she really wants me to live with them. She *said* so, anyway."

What *I* thought was that Pamela's mom was probably feeling guilty as anything for deserting the family, and felt this was the least she could do.

But Brian said, "Doggone it, then, let's party!" So somebody put on a CD, and Mark ordered pizza. Elizabeth ate at least a bite of hers, but I don't know if she ate the rest. We horsed around the pool and shrieked and shouted like we were all having a great time, a wonderful going-away party for Pamela, but no one was enjoying it much. Pamela had been part of our gang so long that losing her was like losing one of our arms.

When I told Dad about it later, he said that her going to Colorado was probably a mistake, but everyone has a right to her own mistakes, and it wasn't likely to be fatal. She'd eventually make new friends, and maybe she'd get along with her mother better than she did with her dad.

For the rest of the week, Elizabeth and I spent as much time with Pamela as we could. Her dad wouldn't do a thing to help her get ready. He said he wanted no part of it, that it was a bad idea. So it was Elizabeth and I who had to help her sort through her stuff—what to take now and what to get later. She said maybe she'd come back for Thanksgiving and take the rest. We filled two huge suitcases with stuff she'd need for school in Colorado, but every little thing seemed to remind her of something she'd done with her friends, and she'd cry.

We tried to make her laugh. "Maybe all this packing will help tone our bodies," I said hopefully, realizing it had been a week since we'd all been running. "I don't know what Elizabeth and I are going to do without you here to get us going in the mornings."

"You'll manage," Pamela said. "No one is indispensable, you know."

Elizabeth sat staring sadly down at the dried corsage that Pamela had saved from the eighth grade semiformal. We remembered the way we went over to Elizabeth's to get ready, how we all went in the same car. Patrick was sick and I went solo, but my friends stuck by me . . . . Now *I* began to tear up. And suddenly all three of us sat there bawling.

"Pamela," I said, my nose clogged. "I never told you, but I'm really sorry about the way I pulled your hair back in sixth grade."

"Pulled her hair?" Elizabeth stared at me. "Why?"

Pamela wiped one arm across her eyes. "Onstage, too," she said.

"*What?*" said Elizabeth again.

"I was jealous," I told her. "I got stuck being a bramble bush because I couldn't carry a tune, and Pamela got the best part—her with her long hair down to her waist, the way she wore it then. When she stepped on my foot, I pulled her hair."

I thought it would make us all laugh, but nobody did.

"Oh, I probably deserved it," Pamela said. "I was all stuck-up, as though the sixth-grade play was the most important thing in the world."

"Promise you'll write?" said Elizabeth. "E-mail us. We'll write each other every day."

Lester had said he'd set me up with an e-mail address on his computer, but our family isn't very high tech, and he hadn't done it yet.

"I'll try to get e-mail," I told her. But I felt we needed something more here. "I think we should each give Pamela something to remember us by, something that means a whole lot to us," I said.

Elizabeth agreed, and we sat thinking. Probably the two most important things in the world that I own are my mom's locket, with a lock of her hair inside, the same color as mine, and the ring with the large green stone that Mrs. Plotkin had given me. I couldn't give either of those away, not even to Pamela.

When we went over to her place the next day, our last evening together, Elizabeth gave Pamela a Saint Agnes card that she said would protect her from rape, because St. Agnes is the saint of bodily purity, having gone through all kinds of tortures to keep herself pure. Elizabeth said it would protect Pamela a whole lot more if she believed in saints herself, but it was better than nothing.

"Do I have to wear it around my neck or anything?" Pamela asked. Both Pamela and I are religious ignoramuses.

"Of course not, but keep it close to you always," Elizabeth told her.

Then I handed Pamela a small envelope. When she opened it, she found the wrapper from a Milky Way bar. She stared at me. "Minus the candy?" she asked.

"It was the wrapper off the first thing Patrick ever gave me," I explained. "It was the first time I realized he liked me."

I think this impressed Pamela more than the Saint Agnes card did because she knows how much I like Patrick. "I'll keep it always," she said. The same thing I'd told Mrs. Plotkin about her ring.

We went back out through the living room, where Mr. Jones sat like a statue in front of the TV set. He hardly said anything to us. Just watched us go in and out of Pamela's room, like a man who had lost his wife and was about to lose his daughter, and didn't know what to do about it.

Because he was so against her leaving, Pamela's mom had sent her a reservation on an afternoon flight, knowing that one of her friends would see that she got to the airport. Mr. Jones would be at work, and there wouldn't be any scenes at the last minute. Lester agreed to drive Pamela to the plane if he could just drop her off and not have to wait around with her. Elizabeth and I went along.

We sat in the backseat together, Pamela in the middle, and alternately laughed and cried, each trying to cheer the others up, but it never worked.

Lester watched us warily in the rearview mirror. "Hey, Pamela," he said finally. "If you come back for Thanksgiving, do we have to go through all this again?"

"Of course," she said. "And you know I'll miss you, too, Lester."

He put his hand over his heart. "And then my heart with pleasure fills, and dances with the daffodils," he said.

"Don't quote Shakespeare to me, Les, it doesn't help," Pamela said.

"Don't you know Wordsworth when you hear it?" Les said.

"As soon as you get there, Pamela, send me an e-mail so we'll know where to write," Elizabeth said as we pulled up at the airport.

"Give us your address when you get a new apartment," I told her.

"Say good-bye to everyone for me," Pamela told us.

We climbed out as Lester got the two huge suitcases from the trunk and gave them to a sky cap. Elizabeth and I broke down again as we hugged Pamela for the last time, till finally the skycap said, "Let's go, miss, before your friend here gets a ticket."

We got in the car and watched as Pamela followed her bags into the terminal. She grew smaller and smaller until she was only a tan shirt and blue jeans. Then all we could see was the reflection of sky in the glass of the revolving door.

13

Marilyn

Dad was leaving for England, and Patrick left before Dad. Everyone seemed to be leaving. If they didn't die, they moved away, and if they didn't move, they were off to England or Maine or some other wonderful place.

Patrick gave me a long, tender good-bye kiss. The thing about Patrick's kisses is that no two are alike. Some are long and intense, some are short little pecks on the cheek, and some are light brushes of lips against lips, tantalizing things that make you want to grab him and hold him and make him kiss you in earnest.

"See you in eighteen days," he told me. He asked what he could bring me from Maine, and I told him a perfect shell.

"I'll try," he said.

I helped Dad pack. That's all I seemed to be doing lately, helping people leave. But I wanted him to look extra nice for Miss Summers. Two whole weeks with the woman he loved without Lester or me around to interrupt—two whole weeks for her without kids from school noticing who she was with.

"Any shirts that need ironing, Dad?" I asked. "Any buttons missing?"

"I think I'm set," he said. "Is there anything in particular you'd like me to bring you from England?"

The perfect mother, I wanted to say. *The news that you and Miss Summers are going to be married.* I didn't say that, of course.

"Choose something," I said. "Whatever you or Sylvia—I mean, Miss Summers—think I'd like." If Dad and Miss Summers *did* marry, I wonder what I was supposed to call her. I certainly wouldn't go on calling her "Miss Summers," but I wouldn't call her Mrs. McKinley, either. How would just plain "Sylvia" be? I'm not sure I could ever call her "Mom."

Dad was taking a cab to the airport because Lester had an exam at school, so I waited with him in the living room until the taxi drove up.

"Have a safe trip, Dad! Have fun!" I said, giving him a long, hard hug. "I love you." What I meant was, *Don't let anything happen to you, because I don't want to be raised by Lester.*

"I love you too, honey," he said. "Hope things go well here at home." What *he* meant was, *I don't want to hear that the neighbors had to call the police.* He gave me a quick kiss on the forehead, and he was gone.

Actually, I was more worried about Pamela at the moment, because Elizabeth had had only one e-mail from her from Colorado, nothing more. I reminded Lester again, when he got home, that I wanted an e-mail address so Pamela and I could write each other.

"I'm not only giving you an e-mail address, babe, I'm going to give you my whole computer. I'm getting a new one this week with a lot more memory."

I screamed and hugged him, and he said if I ever screamed like that again he'd take it back. But that very night he moved it into my bedroom—it took up my whole desk—and set up an e-mail address for me. He showed me how to sign on, how to write a message and send it. He even showed me how to write something and send it to a lot of people at once. Elizabeth had given me a list of the e-mail addresses of some of our friends, so I typed up the news that I now had a computer, and e-mailed my address out to some of the gang. Gwen must have been online at the same time, because I got a message right back: *Hey, girlfriend!*

Welcome to the Age of Technology. I was in.

I wanted to learn to type papers on it, though, so that I could do English assignments when I started high school. Lester gave me the manual, but the word processing program was so complicated! He even had books called *Windows 95 for Dummies* and *Idiot's Word,* but I guess I needed a book for imbeciles in order to figure things out, because I still couldn't get to first base. The margins would jump or the type would dance or numbers would suddenly start appearing down the left side of the page. It was crazy. Lester had given me a computer on the edge of a psychotic breakdown, that's what.

But between his new girl friend, his part-time job at the shoe store, and his summer classes, he didn't have a lot of time to help me, and when Marilyn Rawley called the next evening to ask if I'd heard from Dad, I told her about the trouble I was having with the computer.

"I could come over sometime and do some troubleshooting for you," she said.

"*Would* you?" I begged.

"As long as Lester's not around," she answered.

"Come Tuesday. He's in school all afternoon on Tuesdays," I told her.

"Deal," she said.

• • •

Within a few days of Dad's leaving, Lester and I broke one of the rules, but because we both agreed to it, we figured it was okay. Lester and Eva went to a crafts fair in Frederick on Saturday afternoon, and were going to stop off at a little restaurant on the way back. But the restaurant had closed, and when Lester remembered the leftover fettuccine we'd had the night before when we'd ordered far too much takeout, he brought her here for a little supper.

We both knew that Dad wouldn't mind if they simply ate and left again. What Dad really meant by that "no member of the opposite sex" rule was "nobody of the opposite sex going upstairs." And "no member of the opposite sex lying down on the couch beside you." *Those* kinds of rules.

When Lester brought her inside and explained that they were going to have a quick bite and head for the movies, I knew this wasn't a good time to remind Eva of her promise to do a makeover on me, but I was hoping she'd bring it up again. She had only been in the house for fifteen minutes, however, when I decided I might not like her for a sister-in-law after all.

"This is fettuccine Alfredo?" she asked, pronouncing it with a decidedly Italian accent, rolling the r.

"Supposed to be," Les said, pausing with some

of it wrapped around the end of his fork as though poised for her next comment.

"They obviously didn't use cream," she said. "Fettuccine Alfredo demands cream, or why bother? Cream and great cheese."

Lester said nothing, just popped the forkful in his mouth.

"Tastes good to me!" I chirped. "Pass the fettuccine Alfrrrrredo, Lester, and I'll have some more," I said.

Eva went on picking at her food, pushing the pasta from one side of her plate to the other.

"How was the crafts fair?" I asked Lester.

"Some interesting pottery," he said. "I almost bought a beer pitcher. Had little ceramic figures around the bottom of fat men in a London pub, caps on their heads, knee breeches, the works. Real art."

Eva laughed musically. "Oh, darling, not *art!* Craft, maybe, but not art."

"Folk art, certainly," Lester said. "And better than anything *I* could do."

"Or me, either, but that still doesn't make it art," Eva said with authority.

I looked at Eva. "Define art," I said.

"Well, a craftsman," she instructed, "has the ability to turn out a product of precision and skill. But an *artist* produces a work of such originality and inspiration that it transcends craft. It goes beyond mere talent."

"I still liked the beer pitcher," said Lester. "I would have bought it if I'd had the dough."

The musical laugh again. "If we ever have a bar in the basement, you could keep it there," she said, and gazed at Lester with fond exasperation.

If we ever have a bar in the basement? I couldn't stand the thought of Eva in our family. I couldn't stand the thought of them having a bar. A basement. A house!

And then the world sort of stopped. My breathing did, anyway, because Lester suddenly put down his fork, looked at Eva, and said, "If I have a house, I will buy a beer pitcher and put it any damn place I please."

I stared. Eva stared. Then she gave another little laugh that wasn't quite so musical. "Of course you will, Les! If it's *your* house, you can do anything you want," she said.

The silence there at the table was awesome. It was Lester's cue to say if he ever intended to include Eva in his future, and he didn't exactly jump at the chance. Needless to say, she didn't finish her fettuccine.

When they left, neither was smiling, and I called Elizabeth to come over and make brownies with me. I told her about Lester and Eva, and she said that marriage was a partnership, and everything was supposed to be divided fifty-fifty—money, decisions, chores, worries . . . I wondered if it ever really worked that way, though—if sometimes one partner seemed to be doing all the giving, and another time, the other. Anyway, we mixed up the dough, put half of it on the bottom of a baking pan, put caramels over the dough, then spread the other half of the dough on top. It was our own creation, and nothing Betty Crocker would put in a cookbook, probably, but I thought it turned out okay. It would have been better if we'd melted the caramels first, because there were these huge, chewy lumps all over the brownies, but they were good. Elizabeth even ate one. Well, half a brownie, anyway.

"I still haven't heard any more from Pamela, have you?" she asked.

"Not a peep," I said. "I've sent her three e-mails at the Colorado address, and she hasn't replied. And we never did get her mom's street address because she said they'd be moving soon."

"Do you suppose she's okay?"

"Sure. Probably just trying to get things straightened out, especially if they're moving," I said.

Elizabeth took another brownie, but simply dissected it on her plate, separating the caramel from the chocolate and then not eating any of it. "What if she didn't go to Colorado, Alice? What if she really bought a plane ticket to somewhere else and didn't tell anyone?"

"Her mom sent her the plane ticket, Elizabeth. And we'd have heard by now if she hadn't got there. Her dad would have come over here first thing."

"Oh. Right." Elizabeth was quiet a moment. "Well, what if she went to her mom's, but the mother's boyfriend turned out to be *el creepo* who sneaks in her bed at night and molests her, and she's afraid to tell anyone?"

"Pamela? Are you kidding? She's no eight-year-old dummy! If a man tried to molest Pamela, she'd kick him in the groin so hard, he couldn't walk for a week." I studied Elizabeth. "Are you still planning on being a nun?"

"I'm not sure. Why?"

"I think you ought to write for television instead. I think you should write screenplays for *Homicide* or *Mystery!* or something. Your imagination always works overtime."

"Well, what if another week goes by and we still haven't heard from Pamela?"

"*Then* we'll worry," I said.

We were washing up the mixing bowl and pan when Lester came in. He clomped into the kitchen, ignoring Elizabeth, jerked open the refrigerator door, glanced at the contents, then banged the door again.

"I am through with dyed-haired, made-up, half-starved, ill-tempered, spoiled-rotten, money-hungry, self-centered, know-it-all women!" he declared, as though I had anything to do with Eva. And then he turned on Elizabeth. "Don't ever trade a healthy body for a bag of bones in high heels!" he thundered, and with that he marched back down the hall again and stomped his way upstairs.

Elizabeth stood staring after him, then looked at me. "What was *that* all about? What did *I* do?" she asked.

"You were in his line of fire, that's all," I told her, but I couldn't help smiling. "I think he just broke up with Eva!" And suddenly I yelled, "All riiiiight!" and we gave each other a high five.

After Elizabeth went home, I waited an hour, then went upstairs and knocked on Lester's door. He was playing a CD, so I figured that music had at least calmed the beast.

"Yeah?" he called.

I opened his door a few inches. "I take it you and Eva aren't 'an item' anymore?"

"You could say that," said Lester. He was lying on his bed in his bare feet, reading a mountain bike magazine.

"Are you still hungry? I could fix you something. . . ."

"What are you, my indentured servant?"

"No, I just thought you could use a little TLC."

He gave me a weak smile. "Thanks. Appreciated."

"I never liked Eva, Les, but I didn't want to tell you."

"Well, come to think of it, I didn't, either. She was gorgeous in an artificial sort of way, and sexy as anything, and exciting, and she smelled good. But she was one of the few women I've known who made me feel bad about myself. No matter what I did, it was never right. I couldn't please her in a thousand years."

It was one of the few times Lester had really confided in me, and I started to put in a plug for Marilyn Rawley but decided to keep my mouth shut, and went back downstairs again. As I reached the bottom of the stairs, the phone rang. It was Dad, calling from England. I could hear him as clearly as if he was right across the street. I'd thought his voice would be all garbled, and I'd hear waves sloshing against the telephone cable or something.

"It's Dad!" I yelled to Lester, and he came out into the hall and picked up the phone upstairs.

"So how is everyone?" Dad asked.

"We're fine!" I told him.

"How are things there?" asked Lester.

"We're having a great time," said Dad. "Sylvia has this charming flat, and we've toured Chester and half of England as well. I haven't got the hang of driving on the left side of the street, but you should see Sylvia zip around as though she were born here."

There were a million things I wanted to know, like, were they sleeping in the same bed? But what I said was, "Have you seen any castles?"

"A couple. They're great places to visit, but I'd rather live right back there in Silver Spring. You two getting along okay?"

"Haven't killed her yet," Les replied.

And then Dad was saying, "Sylvia has only one phone in her flat, so I can't put her on at the same time, but we have some news we both wanted to share with you."

I don't think I was even breathing. I don't think Les was, either, because we didn't even say *what?*

"We're going to be married next year."

"Oh, *Dad!*" I yelped in delight.

"Congratulations, Dad! That's wonderful news!" said Lester.

"I'm a very lucky man," Dad told us.

And then, Sylvia's voice. "Hi, Alice! Hello, Lester!

Isn't this exciting? We wanted you to be the first to know."

"I'm so *happy!*" I kept repeating. "I've wanted this forever!"

"Welcome to the family," said Lester.

"Can I tell everyone?" I squealed. "Have you set the date? Is the wedding going to be here in Silver Spring?"

Dad's voice again. "I don't think we'll even need to send out announcements, Sylvia. Just tell Al, and the whole world will know."

"Oh, this is the best!" I kept saying. "Miss Summers, I . . ." I waited till Dad put her on again. "Well, I guess I won't be calling you Miss Summers any more."

"Just call me Sylvia," she said.

I don't even remember saying good-bye. I only remember running upstairs and grabbing Lester and jumping up and down, then turning a backward somersault in the hallway and banging my knee on a door frame. I didn't even care. I felt no pain.

"Anybody got a tranquilizer gun?" Lester said.

"Aren't you *excited*, Lester? Isn't it wonderful? I've wanted this more than anything in the whole wide world, and it's really coming true!"

"I don't think Dad ever sounded happier," Les agreed. "It's about time things started going his way."

I spent the next hour calling everyone I knew, and if they weren't home, I left messages on their e-mail.

Elizabeth was almost as manic as I was. "What if they spend their wedding night right there at your house?" she said.

"Elizabeth!" I said, faking shock. "You wouldn't be talking about *sex*, would you?"

We carried on so long that Lester came out of his room and closed my door. But after I made my last call and put down the phone, I realized I wanted to tell Pamela more than anyone, and I didn't even know where she was.

I didn't tell Lester that Marilyn was coming over Tuesday to help me with the computer. I didn't want him to think I was doing anything to get the two of them back together, and to tell the truth, I simply forgot. All I could think about was that I was finally going to get a mother, and even though I wouldn't call her that, she'd be there for me when I needed her. Finally something good had come out of this long, hot summer.

Marilyn arrived on Tuesday in shorts and a tank top with the outline of her nipples barely visible under the tan cotton. Her long dark hair was piled on top of her head, some hanging in wisps down the back of her neck, and she carried an armload of computer manuals.

It was probably one of the hottest days on record for the Washington area, and our house—an old house—isn't air-conditioned. We've got window units in the living room and Dad's bedroom, but Les and I just open our windows wide at night and hope for a breeze. Dad keeps talking about central air-conditioning, but it hasn't happened yet. You can bet we'll get it before Miss Summers comes here to live.

"My lord, Alice, it's hot up here!" Marilyn complained after I'd told her all the news and we'd worked at the computer for an hour.

I apologized and set up a fan to blow on her bare legs, but even a fan can't blow away Washington's humidity. Marilyn's a good sport, though. Eva probably would have thrown a fit and walked out after the first ten minutes.

She showed me a lot of things—how to make a new document on the computer, and organize stuff into "folders" where I could find them again. She set up school files and friends' files and personal files so that I could put things in their proper place. Most important, she showed me the "escape" key and the "undo" key, and I began to think I could survive the computer age after all.

After we'd been at it for two hours, though, we

were both ready to quit for the day. Marilyn was meeting her sister later at the mall, and she said, "Alice, would you mind if I took a quick shower?" She sniffed her armpits. "I've been sweating like a pig."

"Sure, go ahead," I told her. "I'll get a fresh towel for you." I put one in the bathroom along with a box of body powder I'd got for my birthday, and felt almost as grown up as Marilyn—having an adult woman for a friend. She was so different from Eva. No matter what Eva might have done for me, I never would have felt comfortable around her in a million years.

It wasn't until I heard the shower running that I suddenly remembered that Lester's summer classes were over, and he was on break! He'd had finals! He was through! He was gone, but where he was I hadn't the faintest idea, and I didn't know when he'd be home, either. Maybe, though, he wouldn't come back until Marilyn had left.

No such luck. Marilyn had only been in the shower about two minutes when I heard a car door slam, and the next thing I knew, Lester was standing in the hallway, his gym bag under his arm.

"Where is she?" he said.

Then I remembered Marilyn's car out front. I tried to stay cool. "Marilyn?" I said. "Relax. She came by to help me with the computer, and it's stifling in my room, so she's taking a shower before she meets her sister at the mall."

Lester looked somewhat relieved to know she hadn't come by to see him.

"I forgot your classes were over," I told him. "I thought you'd be gone all afternoon."

"Well, I'm stifling, too," he said. "What have we got to drink?"

"I made lemonade," I said. "Just go out in the kitchen and you won't even have to see her when she leaves."

"Hey, I'm a big boy, Al. I don't have to hide in the kitchen," he said and, as if to prove his point, he stood just inside the living room sorting through the day's mail.

"Suit yourself," I said. I went out in the kitchen and poured us each a glass of lemonade. I was just going back through the hallway when there was a knock at the front door.

I stood there holding both glasses as Lester went to answer. The door swung open, and all we could do was stare.

"Aunt Sally!" we gasped in unison.

14

The Traveler Returns

There she was, all 170 pounds of her, with her suitcase in one hand and her purse in the other.

"We . . . we thought you were in Michigan!" I spluttered.

She smiled and stepped inside with that take-charge manner that makes you want to run for cover. "I know you did, dear, and I didn't want to trouble Lester to come to the airport for me, so I just took a cab here."

"But I thought you told Dad you couldn't come," Les protested.

"Well, I got to thinking about it, and asked myself, *Now what is more important? Another week of fishing with Milt or looking after my sister's children the way I'd promised I would?* I decided I'd done my duty to my husband, and I should spend the other week doing my duty to Marie by coming here and looking after you two, so here I am."

She put her bag down and held out her arms. I can't say we exactly fell into them. We each dutifully hugged her, though, and Lester said, "You know, Sal, I *am* twenty-one. Twenty-two, next month."

"I know, Lester, but I also know that a young man's hormones work overtime in their twenties, and if *I* had a twenty-something son and a fourteen-year-old daughter, *I* wouldn't leave them alone together in the house for one minute."

"What?" I croaked. Did Aunt Sally actually think that . . . that Lester and I . . . that we . . . ?

She immediately blushed. "Oh, I didn't mean *you!* Heavens, no! But . . . Alice with her Patrick, and you, Lester, with your Marilyn, and . . ."

"He's not dating Marilyn," I said. "And Patrick's away for two weeks. We're really doing just fine, Aunt Sally, and Uncle Milt will miss you."

"Uncle Milt can take care of himself," she said, "and I'm not here to interfere in your lives. I'm just going to give the house a good cleaning and do some cooking and baking so that when the traveler returns from England, he'll have a spick-and-span house to come back to, as well as something in the refrigerator."

Lester and I could only exchange helpless looks. You can't exactly tell your aunt you don't want her. You can't tell your mother's sister to leave.

"Now you two just go right on doing whatever you were doing when I got here, and I'll make myself at home," Aunt Sally said. "You don't have to worry about me." She picked up her suitcase and started upstairs.

Dumbly we watched her go. Neither of us could think of what to say, and at that precise moment, when Aunt Sally was three steps from the top, Marilyn Rawley stepped out of the bathroom with a towel around her and called, "Alice, do you have any . . . ?" Her voice tapered off. "Deodorant?"

Aunt Sally stared at Marilyn's bare legs, then turned and looked down the stairs at Lester.

"She's *my* friend," I said, and called, "second drawer on the left, Marilyn."

Marilyn whirled about and disappeared in the bathroom again.

Aunt Sally put her suitcase on the top step and came back downstairs. "Lester, was that Marilyn Rawley?"

"Yes, Sal, it was."

She looked at me. "You lied to me?"

"Aunt Sally, come out in the kitchen and have some lemonade and I'll explain the whole thing," I said. She followed me to the kitchen and sat down, fanning herself.

I gave her my own glass and sat down across from her. I told her that Lester and Marilyn had broken up. I explained how he had given me his old computer, and Marilyn had come over to help me with it, how I'd forgotten that summer classes were over at the university, and Les had come back to find Marilyn here. . . .

Aunt Sally sighed. "I shouldn't have come," she said, subdued.

"No, Aunt Sally, I don't think you should have," I said honestly, "and certainly not without calling first." I teased her a little. "You were trying to check up on us and you know it."

She wrung her hands. "Carol *told* me not to come."

"Smart woman," I said.

"But Ben was the one who suggested it. *He* was the one who called *me*."

"I know. That's because I was hiding Pamela here," I said. And then I had to explain about that.

Aunt Sally took another sip of lemonade. "I can tell that if I stay here till Ben gets back, Lester's going to hate me," she said.

"He won't hate you, but he's not exactly happy. It's *me* he's mad at, for upsetting Dad enough to call you in the first place," I told her.

"So . . . ," Aunt Sally put down her glass. "I tell you what I'm going to do. I'm going to stay just long enough to do some baking and put a few things in the freezer, and then I'm going to change my reservation and fly home."

I smiled.

"I'll get home a few days early so I'll just have time to bake a pie for Milt too," she said.

"Then *everyone* will be happy," I assured her. "You know, Aunt Sally, we're growing up. Lester's an adult now."

"I know. Carol keeps reminding me of that. It's just . . . just that no matter how old your children get, you never stop worrying about them. You won't understand that until you're a mother yourself, Alice, but it's true."

"I suppose so."

"And maybe, because Marie's not here, I feel I have to do her worrying for her."

"Dad can do enough for both of them," I said. And then I remembered the *big* news. "But guess what! He's going to get married! He called a few days ago, and he and Sylvia are marrying when she comes back next year!"

Aunt Sally just stared at me. I don't know what I expected her to do—stand up and cheer, maybe—but she didn't even smile. Just looked at me with such puzzlement that suddenly I knew: I had just announced that the man her sister had been married to was engaged to another woman. And she probably wondered how I, her sister's daughter, could be happy about something like that.

"I guess they really love each other," she said at last.

"I guess so," I said.

"And Marie wouldn't have wanted Ben to be lonely the rest of his life."

"Not if Mom was as wonderful as you say."

"Then I guess I'm happy for him, too, Alice," said Aunt Sally.

We heard the front door close, and when I went out to the living room, both Marilyn's and Lester's cars were gone. I went upstairs to make up Dad's room for Aunt Sally, and then went back down while she settled in. The phone rang. It was Carol.

"Alice, listen, my mother's on her way to your place. Don't ask me to explain, but she feels it's her duty. I *tried* to tell her not to go, but she . . ."

"She's here," I said.

"Oh, my gosh."

"It's okay, Carol," I said, grateful forever to the wonderful cousin who explains a lot of things to me, including sex. "We had a little talk, and she's only staying a couple of days."

"How did you manage *that*?" asked Carol.

"The friendly art of persuasion," I said. "But listen! Have I got news . . .!"

True to her word, Aunt Sally stayed only two days, a dish towel pinned to the front of her dress as an apron, her glasses sliding forward a little on her nose, and her feet firmly planted in white oxfords. She spent the first day baking, the second day cleaning, the air conditioner in the living room and bedroom going full blast, and then she flew back to Chicago.

What I didn't find out until later was that the day she had come, Lester and Marilyn were laughing about it upstairs—the way Marilyn had walked out of the bathroom with a towel around her— and decided to go have ice cream at the mall with Marilyn's sister. They were friends again, Lester told me. Just friends. But I could live with that.

It was fun to e-mail this story around, but I wished Patrick was here so I could tell him in person. I got a postcard from him that afternoon, though: HAVEN'T FOUND THE PERFECT SHELL YET. WILL YOU SETTLE FOR THE PERFECT KISS? SEE YOU SOON.

The day before Dad was due home, I spent the afternoon at Elizabeth's, just talking, hanging out. It was cooler in her room, for one thing, and her mother always fixed something for us to eat when I came over, which was always better than whatever Les and I were eating back home.

What was bothering us both was that there was still no word from Pamela.

"I think it's bad news," Elizabeth said. "When things are going well, you want to tell everybody. When they're not . . ."

She was right about that. "Think we ought to call her dad and see if he's heard from her?" I wondered. "Of course, he'd probably hang up on me, the way I hid Pamela at my house."

"I don't know," Elizabeth said. "She's probably busy getting registered in a new school, and they can't do that until they know where they're going to live."

"I hated to see her go feeling so bad about everything," I said. "In fact, I haven't seen Pamela look happy for a long time, have you? Not since before her mother ran off with that boyfriend."

We lay on the bed idly leafing through magazines.

"How are things with you and Justin? Are you going out at all?" I asked her.

"He hasn't called in a while. We'll see," Elizabeth said, and didn't offer any more.

"Elizabeth?" came her mother's voice suddenly from below. And then, louder, "Elizabeth?"

There were hurried footsteps on the stairs. We jumped up. Had something happened to Nathan?

The door to Elizabeth's room burst open, and there stood Pamela.

We could only stare at first, and suddenly we were screaming and laughing and swarming all over Pamela, hugging and dragging her down on the bed.

"Pamela!" We kept saying her name as though we'd never heard it before.

Mrs. Price was standing in the doorway laughing. "I just answered the door, and there she was!" she told us, and went downstairs again.

"Are you back?" we kept asking Pamela. "Are you staying?" She looked a little heavier than she had before, as though she'd been on a fast-food diet, and she needed a haircut, but we didn't care what she looked like. We just wanted her here.

"I'm back," she said at last, after we'd squeezed the breath out of her. "Mom's boyfriend is a total jerk. I told her so. And she sent me home. If she hadn't, I'd have left, anyway."

"But . . . your dad . . .?" I began.

"I called him from Colorado, and we had a long talk. I told him how I hated it when he said I'd turn out like Mom, and I didn't like him calling me a tramp, either. I said he had to trust me more, and he said I had to let him know where I was going and when I'd be home, and I guess we both agreed to try harder. We're also going to see a counselor. He set it up. So here I am."

"You don't know how good it is to see you!" Elizabeth told her.

"Pamela!" I said suddenly, grabbing her arms. "Dad and Miss Summers are getting married!"

Pamela shrieked. "Honestly? Oh, Alice! You'll be in the wedding!"

"I hope so. It's not till she comes back next year, though."

Pamela stared at me. "You mean she's not coming home right away? She's going to stay in England and *teach*?"

"Well . . . yes. I mean, that's what she agreed to do," I said.

"I thought she went there to be alone and make up her mind! So she's made up her mind. I'd think she'd take the first plane home. She can legally have sex every night if she wants it, and she's going to come back next *year*?"

We sat there on the bed thinking about it.

"Maybe they just like to anticipate it—have something to look forward to," I said at last.

"It doesn't seem any stranger than you going out to Colorado to live, Pamela, and coming back again three weeks later," Elizabeth observed. She studied Pamela's face closely. "What exactly did your mom's boyfriend do to you?"

"He didn't slap me around, if that's what you mean," said Pamela.

That's not what Elizabeth meant. "He didn't sneak in your room at night and . . . and molest you, did he?"

"No, but the kinds of looks he gave me, I felt as

though he'd like to. And Mom didn't even notice," Pamela said. "She's so dense when it comes to her boyfriend. She only sees what she wants to, and makes excuses for him all over the place. I'll bet he's cheating on her and she doesn't even know it."

"That would be so awful," I said. "Your boyfriend making out with someone else and everybody knowing it but you."

"Well, that's mom for you. She ran away with him on impulse and now she has to convince herself she did the right thing," Pamela said.

But Elizabeth was still concentrating on Pamela. "You know," she said, "even if you don't want to tell us, Pamela, there *is* a hot-line number you can call."

"I wasn't molested!" Pamela yelled just as Mrs. Price came in the room with some ice-cream sandwiches.

She stopped and looked around, and then, when Pamela and I cracked up, she said, "Well, that's good to know, Pamela," and left the three of us howling on the bed.

We talked for a long time. I told Pamela about Lester and Marilyn, and about Aunt Sally taking us by surprise. She told us about the plane trip to Colorado, and how she'd had to sit next to this man who kept taking his false teeth out and putting them in his pocket, and then putting them back in his mouth again, and we laughed.

I called home finally to let Lester know where I was, and Pamela called her dad to say she was still at Elizabeth's. We lay across one of Elizabeth's twin beds and talked about all the things that had happened since we'd known each other—the Uplift Spandex Ah Bra, the time the boys tried to throw me in the pool, our trip to Chicago together, and the man who hit on Pamela . . .

But there was too much catching up to do for one evening, and finally Pamela's dad came to pick her up around ten. I walked slowly back across the street, smelling a hint of fall in the air, enjoying a light breeze that meant the end of the heat spell.

I thought about the big things—the really big things—that had happened this summer—Mrs. Plotkin's death; Pamela's running away, then moving to Colorado and coming back again; Dad's trip to England, his engagement; and Lester's breaking up with Eva. Somehow the world of grooming seemed so trivial in comparison. I still wanted to look great and feel good about myself, but I wasn't going to spend a lot of my life worrying about it.

You could have the best body, the shiniest hair,

the clearest skin, great cheekbones and legs, and be as lonely as anything. Look at Pamela. Look at Eva. But life was full of second chances. Pamela was back, and the Three Musketeers were going to start high school together after all.

BE SURE TO READ *ALL* OF
THE ALICE BOOKS

Also check out Alice on the Web at
http://www.simonsays.com/alice
- Join the Alice Fan Club!
- Exchange messages with
  Phyllis Reynolds Naylor!
- Get the latest news about Alice!
- Chat with other Alice fans!
- Enter Alice contests!
- Check out the Alice Books
  reading group guide!

"Naylor's funny, poignant coming-of-age series . . . has continued to serve as a kind of road map for a girl growing up today." —*Booklist*